'This is powerful writing likely to shine in your memory for a long time.'
— EMILY CLEAVER, *Litro Magazine*

'Alison Moore has created an unsettling, seemingly becalmed but oddly sensual, and entirely excellent novel . . . a discomforting and moving portrait of intense loss.'
— ALAN BOWDEN, *Words of Mercury*

'Every word feels earned and precise and right. It all builds wonderfully . . . It is the quiet exactitude of this novel that makes it such a powerful work.'
— BEN DUTTON, *A Literary Life*

'A kind of heartbreaking farce . . . Moore's touch has the sharp penetration of a hypodermic needle.'
— ADAM ROBERTS

'As soon as I had finished it I wanted to re-read it.'
— *stillnotfussed*

'Just superbly written.'
— *Literary Hoarders*

'Deliciously unsettling . . . our sense of inevitable disaster becomes almost unbearable.'
— JENN ASHWORTH, *The Guardian*

ALISON MOORE's first novel, *The Lighthouse*, was shortlisted for the Man Booker Prize and the National Book Awards (New Writer of the Year), winning the McKitterick Prize. Both *The Lighthouse* and her second novel, *He Wants*, were *Observer* Books of the Year. Her most recent novel is *Death and the Seaside*. Her short fiction has been included in *Best British Short Stories* and *Best British Horror* anthologies, and broadcast on BBC Radio 4 Extra. Born in Manchester in 1971, she lives near Nottingham with her husband Dan and son Arthur.

Praise for *The Lighthouse*

'A haunting and accomplished novel.'
—KATY GUEST, *The Independent on Sunday*

'No surprise that this quietly startling novel won column inches when it landed a spot on the Man Booker Prize longlist ... Though sparely told, the novel's simple-seeming narrative has the density of a far longer work ... It all stokes a sense of ominousness that makes the denouement not a bit less shocking.'
—HEPHZIBAH ANDERSON, *The Daily Mail*

'It is this accumulation of the quotidian, in prose as tight as Magnus Mills's, which lends Moore's book its standout nature, and brings the novel to its ambiguous, thrilling end.'
—PHILIP WOMACK, *The Telegraph*

'Ultimately, what drew me into this bleak tale of sorrow and abandonment was the quality of the writing – so taut and economical it even looked different on the page somehow – and so effective in creating a mounting sense of menace and unease. It never flinches ... For such a small volume, *The Lighthouse* actually has a deceptively clever structure which I didn't fully appreciate until the ending, and what an ending it is. I had to think about it, and I like that.'
—ISABEL COSTELLO, *On the Literary Sofa*

Praise for *The Pre-War House and Other Stories*

'Showcases the evolution of a writer who refuses to dilute her stories with artificial light or sentimentality to make them more palatable. There's really no need, when she knows how to make bleakness so thrillingly readable.'
—ISABEL COSTELLO, *On the Literary Sofa*

'There is an insistent, rhythmic quality to Moore's writing, and a dark imagination at work.'
—GENEVIEVE FOX, *The Daily Mail*

'Just as uncompromising and unsettling as *The Lighthouse*.'
—DINAH BIRCH, *The Guardian*

'Beautifully crafted, rendered in a lean, pared-down style that accentuates the stark content.'
— *Metro*

'The tales collected in *The Pre-War House* . . . pick at psychological scabs in a register both wistful and brutal.'
—ANTHONY CUMMINS, *The Times Literary Supplement*

'She creates an atmosphere of discomfort pervaded by that niggling feeling that all is not quite as it should be. Clever stuff.'
—*Lit Nerd*

Praise for *He Wants*

'The best novels are the ones that leave you with a sense of yearning, and in *He Wants*, Alison Moore proves her mastery of the medium . . . As Lewis's desires are revealed, the reader is drawn into a compelling series of regrets, coincidences and reminders that life doesn't often bestow second chances . . . Moore's tightly wreathed prose and assured plotting ensure a bittersweet longing for more once the final page is turned.'
—LYNSEY MAY, *The List*

'Moore is a serious talent. There's art here. There's care.'
—SAM LEITH, *The Financial Times*

'A witty and very moving novel.'
—JONATHAN EDWARDS, *New Welsh Review*

'Brave and rigorous.'
—RACHEL CUSK, *The Guardian*

'Moore movingly mines the aching gap between aspiration and actuality.'
—ANITA SETHI, *The Observer*

'*He Wants* is a funny, touching, life-affirming novel about desire.'
—ANNE GOODWIN, *Annecdotal*

Acknowledgements

MY THANKS TO those who have inspired or enabled any part of this collection, whether by making a comment in the pub one night about winking (that's you, Gillian Collard), by wondering aloud at work about an unresponsive computer (that's you, Ian Perry), by taking me on an exploration of some woods or recalling a World War Two bomb that fell very close to home (that's you, Dad), by taking me to India (that's you, Kevin Ryan), by finding us a holiday apartment with a memorable metal staircase up the outside (that's you, Dan), by having a passport 'taken into safe keeping' whilst working as an au pair (that's you, Jenny Kennedy), and so on. Thanks to everyone who has supported and encouraged me in many and various ways – family and friends and the editors and publishers who have given my stories their stamp of approval. Special thanks as ever to Nicholas Royle, my highly valued agent and editor, to John Oakey for a handsome and clever cover design, and to Jen and Chris Hamilton-Emery at Salt for continuing to be such a pleasure to work with.

'When the Door Closed, It Was Dark' ©2010 by Alison Moore, originally published as a chapbook (Nightjar Press)

'Humming and Pinging' ©2000 by Alison Moore, originally published in *The Marches Literary Prize Anthology 2000*

ACKNOWLEDGEMENTS

'The Machines' ©2013 by Alison Moore, original to this collection

'Wink Wink' ©2000 by Alison Moore, originally published in the Creative Writers' Network magazine, winter 2000

'If There's Anything Left' ©2012 by Alison Moore, originally published online at www.theyellowroom-magazine.co.uk

'Static' ©2009 by Alison Moore, originally published online at www.manchesterwritingcompetition.co.uk

'Sometimes You Think You Are Alone' ©2012 by Alison Moore, originally published in *The Screaming Book of Horror* (Screaming Dreams Press) edited by Johnny Mains

'A Small Window' ©2012 by Alison Moore, originally published in *The Warwick Review* vol.6 #4

'The Smell of the Slaughterhouse' ©2012 by Alison Moore, originally published in *The New Writer* #111

'Helicopter Jean' ©2002 by Alison Moore, originally published in *The New Writer* #53

'Small Animals' ©2012 by Alison Moore, originally published as a chapbook (Nightjar Press)

THE PRE-WAR HOUSE
AND OTHER STORIES

ALISON MOORE

THE PRE-WAR HOUSE

AND OTHER STORIES

SALT

CROMER

PUBLISHED BY SALT PUBLISHING 2016

2 4 6 8 10 9 7 5 3 1

Copyright © Alison Moore 2013, 2016

Alison Moore has asserted her right under the Copyright, Designs
and Patents Act 1988 to be identified as the author of this work.

First published in 2013
This edition published in Great Britain in 2016 by
Salt Publishing Ltd
12 Norwich Road, Cromer, Norfolk NR27 0AX United Kingdom

www.saltpublishing.com

Salt Publishing Limited Reg. No. 5293401

A CIP catalogue record for this book is available from the British Library

ISBN 978 1 907773 50 1 (Hardback edition)
ISBN 978 1 78463 084 3 (Paperback edition)
ISBN 978 1 84471 953 2 (Electronic edition)

Typeset in Neacademia by Salt Publishing

Printed and bound in Great Britain by Clays Ltd, St Ives plc

Salt Publishing Limited is committed to responsible forest management.
This book is made from Forest Stewardship Council™ certified paper.

For Dan and Arthur

Contents

THE PRE-WAR HOUSE
AND OTHER STORIES

When the Door Closed, It Was Dark

IN ENGLAND, IT will be autumn. She imagines the paling sun and the purifying chill, the bare branches and the fallen leaves and the smell of decomposition, the smell of the end of the summer. She longs for short days and early nights, wanting home and hibernation.

She steps from the concrete slabs on to the iron staircase and begins the climb up. She can hardly bear the weight she is carrying, and the rising sun beats down on her.

She remembers her first sight of this place. The taxi, air-conditioned and smelling of pine trees, pulled away, leaving her standing on the slabs beside the block of flats. The paintwork was bruise-coloured and blistered. The midday heat was terrific. There was one flat on each floor, the higher storeys accessed by the iron staircase which zigzagged up the front of the building like the teeth of her mother's pinking shears or a child's drawing of lightning.

She climbed the four flights up to the flat in which she would be staying, carrying her suitcase in one hand and holding on to the railing with the other. Reaching the top, she wiped the sweat from her face with the palm of her hand and smelt the tang of iron on her skin. She knocked on the door and waited. She thought she could hear the baby squealing or screaming.

The door was opened by a woman wearing black, with her head shaved and her hairline low on her narrow forehead.

Offering the woman a damp hand, Tina attempted one of the phrases she had practised in the back of the taxi during the long drive from the airport, even though the family's online advertisement had said, 'Can speak English.'

'I'm Tina,' she said, 'your au pair.'

The woman stabbed at herself with her thumb and said, in her own language, 'Grandmother.'

The shrill noise came again from inside the flat. 'The baby?' asked Tina.

'No,' said Grandmother, and beckoned her inside.

The narrow hallway into which she stepped was packed with sunshine – the wallpaper and the carpet were luridly colourful – but when the door closed, it was dark. She walked down the hallway with the violent patterns unseen beneath her feet, her hand sliding blindly down the wall, the wallpaper rough to the touch, and the screaming filled the hallway.

Climbing the two stone steps up to the kitchen behind Grandmother, she first saw the broad back of a tall man standing beneath a bare lightbulb, and then she saw the pig clamped, shrieking, between his knees. She imagined him leading the pig up the iron staircase, her trotters skidding on the metal steps, and heaving her if she would not climb. She pictured the pig stepping through the front door, on to the brightly patterned carpet, being guided down the dark hallway and up the steps into the kitchen.

Another man was silhouetted against the window. He was sitting on a chest freezer, smoking a cigarette and laughing. Grandmother pointed at him and said, 'Father.' A baby sat beside him in a highchair, watching the man with the pig. Tina could tell they were all family – the men and even the baby had the same narrow forehead and the same broad jaw as the woman. They too had black clothes and shaved heads.

Grandmother turned to the man with the pig and said, 'Uncle.' He looked at Tina, looked her in the eye, but did not smile. He returned his attention to the pig squirming between his legs, picked up a large knife, and then he smiled. He wrestled the pig out of the kitchen and across the unlit hallway into a bathroom, and closed the door. The squealing got louder, and then stopped.

All summer, every evening, she has eaten pork.

On the first night, they had chops. They ate together in the kitchen, and Father fed scraps of meat alternately to the baby and to the dog. The family talked quickly, interrupting and raising their voices over one another. The pace and the dialect and the heavy accent made it impossible for Tina to follow the conversation, and her formal phrases were like wallflowers at a wild party.

She must have been staring at Grandmother when Uncle turned to Tina and said in English, 'There was death in the family,' and he touched his shaved scalp to indicate that this was the custom.

'I'm sorry,' she said, and then, 'So you speak English.'

'Yes,' he said, 'I have a girlfriend in England. She lives in London. Where do you live?'

'I'm from Leicester.'

Uncle pushed away his empty plate and said, 'Tigers.'

'Yes,' said Tina, 'Leicester Tigers,' and she smiled, but he did not. Father lit a cigarette.

She was not due to start work for the family until the

morning. Tired from her journey, Tina excused herself and went to bed early. In the bathroom, the shower curtain was pulled across; she did not pull it back. She washed her face and brushed her teeth quickly, went to her room and shut the door. There was a lock – a keyhole – but no key. Despite the heat, she only half-undressed, and got into bed.

She lay awake for a while, hearing the family talking loudly elsewhere in the house. When she fell asleep, they crept into her dreams – she dreamt that there was someone in her room, standing at the foot of her bed, casting a large shadow on the wall, and the pig was there. It jumped up on to the mattress and lay down, heavy and warm against her body, snorting and snuffling in the dark.

When she woke in the morning, opening her eyes to the strange ceiling, she found that she could not move her legs. She lifted her head and looked down the bed. The dog lay across her shins, nosing noisily at something between its paws. It stayed there watching her with its sad, black eyes, its sopping tongue hanging down, while she dressed, and then it followed her to the kitchen, carrying something in its wet mouth.

In the hallway, she met Uncle and he said, 'Tigers.' She smiled, but he did not.

Grandmother and Father were already in the kitchen when she and Uncle arrived. Tina said, 'Good morning,' sat in the place which had been set for her and looked at the breakfast already on her plate.

'Pig fat,' said Uncle, sitting down to his. 'Eat it.' The dog was chasing a half-eaten snout around the kitchen floor with its nose.

Father lit a cigarette, and Uncle said to Tina, 'You have to clean the bath.' The men left, and Grandmother cleared the table around her, and eventually Tina was alone with the baby. She leaned towards him and said, 'Hello,' first in English and then in his own language. She pulled faces and made animal noises and laughed awkwardly, while the unsmiling baby regarded her.

When the baby was napping in his cot in Grandmother's room, Tina went to the bathroom with Uncle. 'I will show you,' he said, pulling aside the shower curtain and bending his big body down to make a white patch on the side of the cast-iron tub.

Tina, scrubbing at the pig blood and rinsing away the pink foam, with the taste of lard on her tongue and the sting of the cleaning fluid at the back of her throat, felt queasy and light-headed. She sensed Uncle standing behind her in the doorway, watching her. When she finished and straightened up, she turned around to look at him, but nobody was there.

On the third day, she unpacked. She placed her valuables – her money and her passport – in the drawer of her bedside table. She put her clean clothes in the chest of drawers and her laundry in the wicker basket.

Grandmother did the family's washing in a big, metal tub with a corrugated board and a bar of soap, and then she threw the dirty water out of the front door. It dashed on the steps and hit the slabs four floors below, and dried in the sun. The sometimes damp pram was kept at the bottom of the staircase. Every trip out was four flights down and four flights back up carrying the baby. Tina seemed to be forever on those slick steps with the baby in her arms.

Grandmother showed her how to scrub the men's shirts against the washboard, how to hang them out to dry on the lines strung from window to window, and how to cook pulled pork. At suppertime, Father sat down quickly and ate hungrily.

'You made his favourite,' said Uncle.

Grandmother touched her on the arm and said something which Uncle translated. 'She says you can be his girlfriend,' he said, indicating Father, who did not look up from his meal. Tina laughed before she realised that Grandmother was making a genuine proposition. Grandmother spoke again, and Uncle said, 'She says if you do not like him, you can be my girlfriend.' He did not smile.

'But you have a girlfriend,' she said.

'She lives in London,' he said. 'You can live here.'

After supper, after the pork scraps had been scraped into the dog's bowl and the greasy plates had been washed and dried and put away, Tina went outside to watch the day ending. The bone-dry washing hung in the sultry air, the dusk beginning to settle in its folds. Uncle was sitting on the top step of the staircase, eating a bag of aniseed balls. She sat down beside him and asked, 'Where is the baby's mother?'

For a long minute, he did not answer or look at her. He moved an aniseed ball around in his mouth; she heard it clattering against his teeth. He rubbed at the dark circles under his eyes. And then he said, 'She left.'

'She left her baby?'

'She tried to take the baby.'

'Where is she?'

He worked the aniseed ball until it was nothing, and then he looked at her and said, 'She's gone.' He smiled; she saw his teeth, his saliva stained red, and the flash of a flat-cut diamond on his incisor.

'But without the baby?'

'A man must have an heir,' he said. He put another aniseed ball in his mouth and did not look at her again.

She wondered about the diamond; she wondered whether it rubbed against the inside of his lip, and whether it hurt. She could almost taste the blood.

Every other evening, when the baby was asleep, Tina had a bath. She took very little hot water, not wanting an incomprehensible scolding from Grandmother, nor a comprehensible one from Uncle. She sat in the deep tub with lukewarm water lapping at her bare knees, bathing warily. There was no lock on the bathroom door. At first she pulled the shower curtain across, in case anybody should come in by mistake, but she found that she preferred to leave the curtain drawn back, so that she could see there was nobody there.

Halfway up the iron staircase, she pauses. She stands still, her arms aching, her legs shaking, nausea swelling in her stomach. She listens to the distant buzz of life, the sounds coming from the market and the factory – a noisy, windowless box of a building in which Uncle works on the production line. She has often wondered what it would be like to spend so much of your life like that, without daylight, without sunshine, without fresh air. The night shift has ended and the day shift has started, and Uncle will be home soon. A mile away, the road is choked with cars and buses, and the streets are full of people coming and going. But here, now, it is dreadfully quiet.

They watched her as she went about the house. They were watching when she went out and they were watching when she returned.

She went to the kitchen to make Father a cup of tea and found Grandmother and Uncle in there. While she filled and boiled the kettle, and fetched a cup and saucer from the cupboard, and made the sweet, black tea, she felt their eyes on her back, felt their gaze following her as she carried the full, hot cup slowly across the kitchen and down the steps. She recalled reading somewhere that if a woman is carrying a cup of tea down the stairs and falls, she won't drop the cup because she will think it's a baby. As Tina stepped carefully from the bottom stair into the hallway, Uncle, close behind her, said, 'She wants to know if you have children.' Tina turned, and the cup rattled on its saucer.

Tina looked at Grandmother, who was standing behind Uncle in the kitchen doorway looking at her, at her figure, at her hips.

'No,' said Tina. 'No children.'

Grandmother spoke, and then Uncle said, 'But you can have children, yes?'

Tina hesitated, thrown, but she said, 'Yes,' although she wondered how she would know – she didn't know that she *couldn't* have children.

In the living room, she gave the cup of tea to Father and he watched her pick up the baby, who smelt of cigarettes.

She gave the baby a bath in the big tub, crouching on the concrete floor, while Grandmother sat on the toilet seat lid with a towel, looking at her. It made Tina nervous, being stared at like that. Grandmother's gaze made her clumsy, made the baby feel particularly slippery and squirmy. He tipped out of the cradle of her arm and headbutted the surface of the water before she righted him. Grandmother stood quickly and, scolding her, intervened, taking the baby out of the bath, out of Tina's hands. She wrapped him in the towel and jiggled him up and down, and he began to cry. Tina drained the shallow bath, and the baby's jagged crying became screaming, scratching at her raw nerves.

One evening, carrying a full glass of water down the kitchen steps, Tina stumbled. The heavy, cut-glass tumbler fell out of her hand, clipped the stone step and whumped down on the carpet, where it lay in the dark puddle of its own spillage. She inspected the glass, and found a crack. There was nobody around – nobody in the hallway, nobody in the kitchen. Tina dried the wet patch on the carpet as best she could and put the glass at the back of the cupboard, behind the rest of the tumblers.

Later, walking through the market, stopping to look at a stall full of glassware, she saw some tumblers very similar to Grandmother's, though not quite the same. She decided she would buy one and secretly replace the one she had dropped, but when she looked in her purse she found she had only small change. She went back to the flat to fetch more of her money, but when she opened the drawer of her bedside table it was empty, her valuables gone.

She went to confront Grandmother, who pretended not to understand her, dismissing her with a flicking, shooing hand. Tina turned to Uncle, who said, 'We will keep safe your money and your passport.' Tina tried to argue, to insist that they return her possessions, but Uncle calmly repeated, 'We will keep safe the valuable things.'

She sat quietly through supper, her stomach knotted, unable to eat. She did not know what she could do, apart from going into their bedrooms to look for her belongings, but there was always someone in the house.

When everyone had finished, Tina cleared away the dirty dishes, scraping the uneaten pork from her plate. Grandmother and the men remained at the table, talking and watching her. Tina washed up. She did not care now about the glass she had broken and hidden in the cupboard. She handled the cut-glass tumblers roughly – they clinked in the water and squeaked in her wet hands in mid-air. Grandmother spoke sharply to Uncle, who said to Tina, 'They are heirlooms. They are valuable.' He thumped his fist twice against his big chest, against his heart, to suggest their sentimental value.

Tina dried the glasses and opened the cupboard to put them away, and immediately she could see that the one she had pushed to the back was gone.

'We must say, Tina,' said Uncle, 'when we make a mistake.'

She put the baby to bed, lingering long after he fell asleep. She couldn't bear to go back to the smoky, suffocating kitchen. Her top was wet under the armpits. Her back and her scalp were sweating. She went to the bathroom, ran the cold tap, and splashed lukewarm water on her face. She opened the tiny window wide, hoping for a little air, but instead she felt the day's warmth slumping through like dead weight.

She nears the top of the iron staircase, and now she is climbing so slowly but still she is almost there.

She went from the bathroom to her bedroom and stopped outside the door. She looked back towards the kitchen, where they were all busy talking, and then stepped across the hallway and slowly opened Grandmother's bedroom door. The baby was asleep in his cot, with his night-light on. She crossed the quiet room, hearing the noise of the carpet beneath her feet. She went first to Grandmother's bedside table and opened the drawer, but inside there was just a Bible. She slid her hand under the mattress and ran it all the way down to the foot of the bed, feeling the bare slats. Under the bed, there were only slippers; in the chest of drawers there were only clothes.

Tina went to the cot. She slipped her fingers down between the bars and the baby's mattress. The baby sighed and Tina froze, willing him not to wake, not to cry – she did not want Grandmother coming down the hallway. She wondered whether she dared to look in the room the men shared. She could still hear the debate going on in the kitchen.

Suddenly, she looked up. A figure stood in the doorway, looking at her with her hands in the baby's cot. Her heart bucked inside her chest like a wild horse roped.

'I was just checking on the baby,' said Tina, and her voice sounded strange to her, disembodied in the dim room.

'My mother does not like you,' said Uncle, the diamond glinting on his tooth as he spoke. 'She does not trust you.'

Tina wondered how long he had been standing there.

'I want my things back,' she said.

'You do not need your passport now,' he said. 'But I will bring you money.'

Tina went to her room and sat on the edge of her bed. When there was a knock at her door, she went and opened it. Uncle held out a couple of notes in the local currency, just pocket money. She looked at him, and he said, 'It is enough now. Why do you want more?'

She took the notes, and closed her door again.

It was so hot. It was unbearable. The window in her room did not open; the frame appeared to have been painted shut. But it seemed that there was no cool air anyway, anywhere. Her heart was beating fast and she felt nauseous. Her mouth was dry; she wanted a glass of water but she did not want to leave her room. She got into bed and lay awake, sweating into these strangers' sheets, loathing the dragging summer, just wanting it to end.

In the morning, she took the baby out early, and quietly, leaving Grandmother sleeping. She walked him slowly through the market while it was setting up, and through the still-calm streets, delaying her return. He fell asleep, and she thought that she would have liked to just keep walking, walking with the dozing baby, never to go back.

She stopped at a payphone and thought of calling her parents. She had coins, or she could reverse the charges. She put the brake on the pram, lifted the receiver, and dialled the international number. It rang – she saw the phone at home ringing in the empty kitchen, ringing through the dark house, because, she realised, if it was early morning here then it was very early at home, still nighttime. She pictured her parents asleep in their bed, or half-woken, frowning into their pillows and turning over. She stood with the receiver pressed to her ear long after she knew that nobody was going to answer.

She heard the factory whistle blow, signalling the end of the night shift. Now Uncle would go drinking, and then he would return home for breakfast.

She replaced the receiver and collected her returned coins. She walked back through the market, and saw the glassware stall again. She had her pocket money from Uncle in her purse. She stopped and looked at the cut-glass tumblers which were not too different from the one she had damaged. She bought one, as a peace offering, and then she walked slowly back to the flats.

She parked the pram on the wet slabs underneath the iron staircase. Grandmother was up – she had done a wash already. Damp laundry hung in the morning sunshine. Tina lifted the sleepy baby out of the pram and began the climb up to the top. She felt queasy at the thought of sitting down to breakfast. She had no appetite. She had a twitch under her eye.

She was more than halfway up when she realised she had left the glass from the market in the bottom of the pram. Wanting to give it to Grandmother before breakfast, she started back down, down the slick steps with the baby in her arms, and perhaps it was because she had not slept or eaten; perhaps it was because she felt sick and was too hot; perhaps it was because she was hurrying, not wanting to meet Uncle on the stairs, smelling of alcohol and aniseed; but in any case, she tripped.

At the top of the staircase, she takes the weight in the crook of one arm and, with a deep breath, opens the door with her free hand. She steps into the bright hallway and pulls the door to behind her, and when the door closes, it is dark.

Humming and Pinging

WE ARE LIKE my Nana and Grandpa, the way we are sitting there, just quietly sitting, saying not a word. They can sit and sit, with the clock chiming every quarter hour, and every now and again Nana will say, 'Perhaps we'll have a cup of tea,' or, 'I'll think about supper soon,' and Grandpa will say, 'Right-o.'

Leanne's my best friend, but today she hasn't a thing to say to me. I say, 'Shall we play something?' but she shakes her head. She's pretending to read a comic but she isn't turning any pages and it doesn't take that long to read a few speech bubbles and thought bubbles, a few *Thump!*s and *Thwack!*s and *Kapow!*s. I say, 'Can I read that with you?' and she shrugs her shoulders but that means no. I sit for a few minutes more, folding the boy band faces on her duvet so that they become one-eyed, no-nosed, pursed-mouthed.

I say, 'Shall I go then?' and she shrugs again, but this time she means yes. I say, 'I'll call for you tomorrow morning then.' She doesn't say or do anything for a moment, but then she nods. 'OK then,' I say, and then, 'Right-o,' to make her laugh. She's sat with me at my Nana and Grandpa's before, and when Nana says, 'Shall we have some telly on?' and Grandpa says, 'Right-o,' we say, 'Right-o,' and sit shaking with the giggles. But Leanne's having none of it today. I put my shoes on and say, 'Ta-ra,' and she says, 'Ta-ra,' back to me, so we're still friends.

It's quiet downstairs too. In the kitchen I say, 'Ta-ra,' to Leanne's mum. She says, 'Goodbye, Carla, see you tomorrow.' I run home, down the road, sixty houses, sixty even numbers, from 128 to 8. I can run all the way but I usually get a stitch by the time I reach the bend in the road where the weeping willow is.

Nana and Grandpa are still up. It's only eight and they don't go to bed until nine or sometimes ten. When I lived with my dad, he went to bed at midnight or after – I knew because I would hear the clock chime and then he would check the doors and switch off the lights and come upstairs. Now he lives in Australia and I live with my Nana and Grandpa and Ruth, my sister.

Ruth's older than me – really too old to be living with her grandparents. She says that and so does Leanne's mother, but Ruth says it's because they cramp her style whereas Leanne's mother says it's because Ruth stays out too late and makes Nana and Grandpa worried and tired.

Nana says, 'We'll have some milk then, shall we?' and Grandpa says, 'Right-o.' Nana and I go through to the kitchen to make it. She heats it up on the hob, and I fetch the cups and cut up the bread to put in Grandpa's. We all have our milk different. We sit in the lounge, Grandpa eating his pobs with a spoon, Nana drinking her cocoa, and me with my milk 'neat' as Grandpa calls it. Nobody says anything much and the clock chimes the quarter-hours away until nine-thirty, and then Nana says, 'Shall we head to bed?' and Grandpa says, 'Right-o.' I run ahead because I'm fastest in the bathroom. I can do my ablutions in four minutes flat, but Grandpa takes an age even though it sounds as if he's just standing still in there, every once in a while coughing and making the floorboards creak.

I have already been asleep when I hear Ruth come in. Sometimes I am woken in the early hours by her boyfriends' noisy old bangers revving and farting outside our house before they finally drive away. But tonight, I only stir when I hear her trying to be quiet closing the door and coming up the stairs, forgetting to miss the squeaky steps. In the bathroom she flushes the toilet, and all the plumbing starts humming and pinging. I know she's woken Nana and Grandpa up because as soon as she's closed her bedroom door I hear them go to the bathroom one after the other, and then I hear Grandpa coughing for half an hour after.

At breakfast they curse the creaking of the stairs and the humming and pinging of the pipes; they say that in the early hours there's nothing that keeps you awake more than that. Ruth picks through her scrambled eggs, and Nana says that Ruth needs to go to bed earlier. Ruth says that she doesn't need much sleep, and Nana says, 'No, maybe not, but look at *my* eye-bags.'

Nana comes to the door with me and leans down to let me kiss her cheek. I say, 'Ta-ra,' and she says, 'Ta-ra,' and I go off up the road to Leanne's.

Her dad is coming out of the house when I get there, which is not the usual thing. Normally Leanne's mum lets me in and sits me down at the kitchen table to wait for Leanne, who's always ages getting ready. Her father will sit there and have just one more piece of toast and just one more cup of coffee and then just one more until he's late and has to rush to work. It's nice in their kitchen in the mornings, but not today.

Today there's nobody in there, and it's cold. The kettle's boiled but there's only his cup, and propped against the wall is a camp-bed. Leanne shouts for me to go upstairs, and as I pass her parents' bedroom I see her mother sitting on the end of the bed. I know she smokes, but I have never seen her smoke in the house before, because Leanne's father doesn't like it. But today she is smoking in the house, on their bed, in her dressing gown.

While Leanne finishes getting ready, I look out of her window. I watch her father climbing into his new red car. When he got it, Leanne's mother said who was he trying to impress with such a big flashy car? He starts the engine and rolls smoothly out of the driveway and onto the street.

We walk to school.

I say, 'Have you got a visitor?'

'What?' says Leanne.

'Have you got someone staying over? I saw the camp-bed.'

'Oh,' says Leanne, 'Dad snores. Mum wanted a good night's sleep.'

'Oh,' I say, 'Right.'

'What's that supposed to mean?' she says, and I flinch.

'Nothing. I just mean, fine.'

'Glad you think so,' she says.

We walk on awkwardly. I would like to start again, to say, *Have you done your maths homework? What have you got first thing?* I would like not to have mentioned the camp-bed.

I say, 'Have you done your maths homework?'

She says, 'I suppose you think your family's just perfect, don't you?' She pauses, but not long enough for me to think of an answer. 'But your mum didn't want you and your dad didn't want you and your grandparents just want some company till they die.'

'Leanne!' I say, horrified.

'Oh, piss off,' she says. She has seen some other girls in our class, and she runs on ahead, leaving me crumpled and unhappy.

They have to wait at the pedestrian crossing, and I panic as I draw near, willing the lights to turn red and allow them across ahead of me, but they don't. I stand behind them and wish I hadn't asked about the camp-bed.

Before the lights have changed, Leanne has bad-mouthed me, Ruth and my grandparents, and it's this last that makes me the most miserable. I try to stick up for them, to stop her mocking their slippers, the stairlift, the pobs and false teeth and early bed-times, but she just talks louder and louder until I let it go. I drop so far back that I arrive at school late and get told off. There is no note-passing in class or sandwich-swapping at lunch-time, and at the end of the day I walk home alone.

'Not seeing Leanne tonight?' Nana asks.

'No,' I say. 'Not tonight.'

'Shall we have some telly on then?'

Grandpa says, 'Right-o.'

I don't answer. I knot myself up in an armchair and we watch *Coronation Street* while Nana worries about my spine.

Later, she says, 'We'll have some milk then, shall we?'

Grandpa says, 'Right-o.'

I say, 'No, thanks.' Both she and Grandpa look up at me, startled. I relent. I drink my milk, neat, and then we head to bed. Nana tries to bustle me up the stairs playfully, and I am resistant at first, not at all playful; but I see her become sad, and so I smile, I laugh, I run ahead and into the bathroom to do my four-minute ablutions before jumping into bed and pulling the starched white cotton sheets up to my chin. Nana comes and kisses me goodnight, and then leaves me in the dark and quiet room listening to the sparse and gentle traffic on the street beneath my window.

Tonight, I can't sleep. I sit up and watch the comings and goings outside. Had I been asleep, I would not have been disturbed by the car that brings Ruth home, that purrs and rolls smoothly to a stop. This car is not a noisy old banger; it is new and red, big and flashy.

There is a long, slow kiss before Ruth climbs out and adjusts her clothing. The driver pulls away, sneaking off up the street and disappearing around the bend where the weeping willow is.

While the stairs creak beneath Ruth's feet, I slip back down under my covers and listen to Ruth and then Nana and then Grandpa making the plumbing hum and ping, and in the early hours there's nothing that keeps you awake more than that.

The Egg

WILLIAM STANDS AT the window, looking out through the snow-speckled glass. There was no summer to speak of, and now, already, it is winter. The first frost arrived overnight, and now the snow. In the small garden, and over the wall in the sprawling park, on the heath and the paths and the frozen lake, it is starting to settle.

Water drips from his damp hair, the greyed remains of it, trickling down the neck of his dressing gown. He looks down at his bare feet, at the blue veins in his winter-pale and water-softened skin, at his bloated ankles, their waxy appearance. They do not look like his; they look like somebody else's.

In the bathroom, his wet footprints are already evaporating from the tiled floor.

The boy was in the park, standing in the wet grass, when William went into the garden to fill the bird table. He watched the boy bending and picking up a stone, holding it in both hands and inspecting it, and then dropping it back into the long grass.

William, standing on his lawn with his hands full of left-overs, said, 'Have you lost something?'

The boy looked up at him, came closer and stood near the gate, resting his hands on the low wall, on the damp stones. His canvas shoes were soaked and his trousers were wet around the ankles as if the water were climbing his legs.

Under the gate, by the boy's feet, there was a puddle full of dead leaves.

Downstairs, William makes breakfast, cutting the rind from the bacon and cracking an egg into a bowl, finding a blood spot in the yolk. His bare feet chill on the kitchen's cold stone floor. The snow is falling densely now, settling on the windowsill, pressing up against the windowpane. There is no traffic on the road behind the cottage, and nobody in the park. It is almost silent; any sound is muffled. William whisks his egg.

On the table, there is a shard of rock. He looks at it while he drinks his coffee.

He takes the rinds and crusts out to the bird table, gazing out at the trees, at their cold, bare limbs, and up at the empty sky, looking for the birds.

There are pigeons on the roof. He hears them in the night, the scrabbling and scratching of their claws on the slate. There are geese and swans in the park. There is bird mess spattered and encrusted on the sandstone; there is dark green slime on the grass.

Not much has changed about the sandstone cottage since he was a boy. The garden is just the same, the grass a little long, the shrubs a little overgrown. On the front door there is a lion's head knocker. When William was little he liked to touch it, tracing the cold curves of the lion's face. In the hallway, by the door, are his mother's shoes with mud still on the heel, as if she has just stepped out of them, as if they would still be warm inside. In the living room, her vinyl is stacked by the record player, a favourite on the turntable. Her clothes, hanging in the wardrobe in the master bedroom, smell of mothballs.

The boy moved his hands from the cold coping stones into the deep pockets of his duffel coat. The coat was the colour of holly berries and made William think of winter.

'How old are you?' asked the boy.

William, turning to drop the bacon rind and the toast crusts onto the bird table, said, 'Shouldn't you be in school?'

'It's the holidays,' said the boy.

William spread the birds' breakfast more evenly over the table.

'I'm going to find a fossil,' said the boy.

'You'll be lucky,' said William.

'I bet I can,' said the boy. He took his hands back out of his pockets, lifted the flap of the satchel he wore across his chest and reached inside. He took out a shard of rock and showed it to William. 'I found this,' he said.

William moved towards the boy to look at the rock, the suggestion of a body in the stone. 'You collect fossils?' he said.

'I've only got that one,' said the boy, returning it carefully to his otherwise empty satchel.

William turned and began his careful walk back up the wet path towards his front door.

'You're older than my granddad,' said the boy, 'and he's dead.'

William, slowly stopping, turning back, said to the boy, 'I've got a collection.'

He had wanted to be a natural historian. He had imagined

23

working in a museum, sitting in a back room, labelling acquisitions. He had not got on at school though. He was bullied, and often his mother had said he did not have to go. 'We'll say you're sick,' she had said, settling him at the kitchen table to draw his birds.

He had missed a lot of school. He never even applied for a museum job, has never even been to the Natural History Museum, but he has his annotated sketches of birds pinned to his bedroom walls, and he has the skeleton of a bird in a jar beside his bed, and he has his collection.

As a boy, William climbed trees, climbed up to the roof of the house, looked in tree stumps and under bushes and in the reeds around the lake, finding nests and taking eggs, just one from each nest, just one of any type: a sparrow's brown and blotchy egg, a blackbird's pale turquoise and brown-speckled egg, a pigeon's white egg.

In William's hands, a warm egg turned cold. Beneath the thin, crackable shell, an immature bird, with embryonic eyes closed, grew still, trapped in its watery environment, suspended like an insect in amber.

In his bottom drawer, underneath his jumpers, there was a large shoebox, and it was full of birds' eggs: a starling's pale blue egg, a thrush's bright blue and black-spotted egg, a robin's white and red-spotted egg.

One day, he came in from the garden, into the kitchen, and found his mother sitting at the table with his shoebox out, the lid off, his stolen eggs in her hands: a yellowhammer's white and purple-scribbled egg, a skylark's greyish and brown-freckled egg, a reed bunting's pale lilac and black-blotched egg.

'What's all this?' she asked him.

William looked at the box, picked out an egg and began to tell her the name of the bird which had laid it, where he had found the nest, how many eggs had been in it.

'These are not yours, William,' she said, taking the egg from his hand, putting it back in the shoebox and taking the shoebox away.

He stood at the window, watching her standing outside, unable to put the eggs in the bin. In the end she pushed them gently under the bush beneath the kitchen window, as if, in the right habitat, they might still hatch.

Later, when he crept down from his bedroom to take the eggs back out from under the bush, his mother was watching. In the garden, on his knees, his head down while his hand groped, he turned and saw her coming towards him. He had not had time to get to his feet before her soft hand flew out and smacked the side of his head so hard he lost his balance, and before he had regained it another blow landed. It all happened so quietly, but he can still feel the smarting and flushing of his skin; he can still see the glare of her small, dark eyes.

When he looked again, she had moved the eggs and he had to start his collection from scratch, with a new hiding place.

William knelt down and retrieved the shoebox from under his bed. He lifted the lid and showed the boy the eggs nestling inside, amongst the balls of cotton wool: a kingfisher's roundish white egg, a coot's buff and brown-spotted egg, a tufted duck's olive-coloured egg. Each one was labelled in a child's handwriting on a small strip of paper pinned to a cotton wool ball.

The boy was impressed. He said, 'There can't be any you haven't got.'

'I haven't got a swan's egg,' said William.

'Why not?' asked the boy.

William had always wanted one, but he was scared of swans. He was afraid of their big, heavy bodies, their powerful wings, their serpentine necks, the hard snap of their beaks, their hissing and biting. And he was especially afraid of nesting swans, which were ferociously protective of their eggs. He had seen their huge nests on the shore of the lake and on the island, but he had never got close to one. There was one on the island which had been there since the spring, abandoned with an unhatched egg inside it. He had watched it through his binoculars.

'They're not easy to come by,' said William, looking down at the boy, at the small, dark head bent over the shoebox. 'You'd be lucky to get one.'

He imagines the first chilly moment of clambering into the lake, the cold water perhaps only up to the knees at first, or up to the tops of the thighs or just above the waist. He imagines the struggle through the reeds, the effort, half-wading, half-swimming and then actually swimming through the icy water to the island. He imagines the swans, which have not left the lake, which have remained into the winter, witnessing the taking of the egg from the nest. He imagines the plunge back into the lake, the body already numb with cold and exhaustion, encumbered by waterlogged clothing and by the bag in which the egg has been stowed, and again the almost-swimming, the struggling in the reeds.

THE EGG

The shoebox is on William's pillow with the lid off. He sits down beside it, holding a tiny rectangle of white paper and a pin. He touches the smooth, cool shells of the eggs: the pale green egg of a mallard; the creamy egg of a goose; a large, light-grey egg beneath which he positions his label, pushing the pin through the paper and through the cotton wool. The tip slides into the soft pad of his thumb, and the blood is slow coming to the surface. The handwriting is scratchier, shakier, than on the other labels. The still-wet ink says, *Mute swan*.

He replaces the lid on the shoebox and pushes it back under his bed.

He had imagined a wife, but it never happened. The master bedroom is vacant now, but his single room suits him fine; he has never used the double bed.

He rarely leaves the house. His shopping is delivered by a Tesco van and brought into his kitchen in a plastic crate which is then taken away again, empty.

But every morning, before his bath, before his breakfast, before feeding the birds, William walks around the lake. He goes early, when it is barely light, so that he will have it all to himself. It is three miles all the way around, and these days it takes him a while. Often he walks the whole way just looking at his shoes and he doesn't even notice the changing seasons. Other times he sees things.

This morning he saw the frost.

He saw the puddle by the garden gate frozen over, the dead

leaves trapped, the ice cracking under his heel as he walked out.

He saw the emptiness of the park beneath the blank dome of the sky, and the snow beginning to fall.

He saw the overwintering swans in amongst the reeds, and the empty nest on the island.

He saw something in the water, near the bank, holly berry red under the snow-mottled ice, and the frosted grass beside the lake crushed beneath his feet.

Overnight Stop

MONICA IS APPROACHING the check-in desk when her phone begins vibrating in the pocket of her shorts. She takes the call, rolling her eyes at Michael. 'Dad,' she says, 'stop worrying. We'll be fine.' She listens briefly before saying, 'I've got to go.'

She and her dad watched *Lost* last night, watched Flight 815 break apart in his darkened living room. After switching off the television, he said to her, 'What time's your flight?'

He is worried about the engines failing, the wings falling off, about terrorists and aggressive passengers, about pilots having heart attacks or falling asleep in the cockpit.

Monica has spent this afternoon sweating into her wedding dress. Now in her holiday clothes, she's a bit cold, and there are hours of in-flight air conditioning which must be endured before reaching the honeymoon destination.

On the far side of check-in, they find somewhere to sit and Monica tries not to think about the wings coming off. Her dad's anxiety seems to be catching, like something she has just discovered growing in her skin, like the itchy ringworm she picked up after scrubbing an infected cage at the veterinary surgery. Her arm, bare between her rubber glove and the sleeve of her bottle-green uniform, must have touched the cage, or perhaps the invading fungal spores were airborne.

'What's wrong with your legs?' says Michael, and Monica

stands to look at the backs of her knees where she has been absent-mindedly scratching.

'What the hell?' she says, still raking her nails over the rash which has broken out.

'It could be the new car seat covers,' says Michael. 'Some people are allergic to neoprene. I'll see if I can get some antihistamines.' He wanders away. When he returns with a bag from the pharmacy, he says, 'Our flight's delayed.'

Monica swallows a tablet. Five minutes later, she says to Michael, 'It's not working.' After another five, she says, 'If anything, it's getting worse.' She is agitated.

Michael is restless too, impatient to be crossing the tarmac and strapping himself into his seat on the plane, to be accelerating down the runway, to be tens of thousands of feet in the air.

They listen to announcements they can't decipher, and Michael goes to investigate. When he comes back and says to Monica that they won't be flying out until the morning, she feels herself relaxing. But then, she thinks, if something dreadful is going to happen, it has only been postponed.

They are going to be put up overnight, says Michael, in an airport hotel.

'Oh well,' says Monica, 'that might be nice.'

They pick up their hand luggage and make their way to the assembly point, from where they and dozens of others will be taken by bus to the hotel.

Walking into the softly lit lobby, looking around at the sofas and potted plants, Monica says to Michael, 'Let's just stay here. We'll stay in our room until it's time to go home. We'll order room service.'

She stops to have a good go at her rash while Michael goes to reception. Hearing the receptionist say, 'Mr and Mrs Porter,' Monica glances up, looking around for Michael's parents before realising that the receptionist is talking about Michael and her. She meets the eye of a thin man with a shaved head who is waiting in line with the other passengers, and then Michael steps away from the desk with keycards in his hand and Monica follows him.

As they walk together to the stairs, Monica is aware of the loudness of her wooden wedges on the tiled floor. She wishes she had worn something quieter, and that she had put overnight essentials in her hand luggage. She could do with a toothbrush and a change of underwear, things that are packed in her suitcase along with her bikinis, her evening wear, a beach towel that says 'OCEANIC TRANQUILLITY' in big, red capital letters, and an alarm clock that will go off in the morning and might be thought to be a bomb. She would like a magazine to read.

When Monica reaches the foot of the stairs, she glances back at the thin man who has now reached the front of the queue and is talking to the receptionist.

I *know him*, she suddenly thinks, and stares for a moment longer before turning away and carrying on up the stairs.

When Monica sees their room, she says again, 'Let's just stay here.' She closes the curtains and lies down on the double bed, discovering that it is two twin beds pushed together, with an unclosable gap between the mattresses. The bedspread irritates her rash.

Michael helps himself to a Malibu from the mini-bar. 'Tomorrow evening,' he says, 'we'll be eating red snapper from the Caribbean.'

'Unless there's still a problem with the flight,' says Monica.

'Twelve hours from now,' he insists, 'we'll be on the plane, strapped into our seats, awaiting take-off.'

Monica goes for a bath. She sits in hot water scrubbing at her rash with a complimentary flannel. She washes her stomach. Her pregnancy is beginning to show. When she gets out, she puts her dirty clothes back on and goes to see if she can get a toothbrush from reception.

The receptionist produces a dental kit and a list of other items the hotel can provide – combs, shaving kits, deodorant, sanitary products, manicure kits, condoms, slippers, shoe polishing kits. Glancing at Monica's clothes, she also mentions the laundry service, and Monica enjoys the thought that she really could manage here for weeks without her luggage.

She wanders over to the lounge area, picks up a magazine and sits down in an armchair.

She is reading a scathing review of a book she liked when she becomes aware of a man standing in front of her. She glances up, expecting to see Michael.

'Hello, Mrs Porter,' says the man.

She recognises him as the one from the queue, the thin man who watched her scratching furiously at her legs while Michael was checking in. She is sure now that she knows him quite well but can't think where from. He watches her struggling to place him and chooses not to help her. He sits down, and as he is getting comfortable it dawns on her who he is and her stomach sinks.

'Well, Monica,' says Stanley, 'Barbados here we come, eh?' He smiles.

He looks different, bared without his long hair and his beard, but he always did smile a lot, although Monica could never decide whether he was friendly or hostile.

She shared a house with a friend of his and never knew if she would return from work to find Stanley on the sofa, drinking milk from the carton, resting it between his thighs after swigs, looking at her in her uniform and saying, 'Hello nursey.' Sometimes, she would feel agitated in anticipation of finding Stanley in the house with the milk between his legs, but then, arriving home, she would find the house empty, the milk untouched in the fridge.

Sometimes, she would come home after a night out to find that he had bolted the front door before falling asleep on the sofa, so that she could not let herself in with her key. She remembers hammering on the door with her fist, trying to wake him, furious that he should have the power to shut her out of her own home.

One time, Stanley wasn't there when she went to sleep, but when she got up at dawn to make coffee, she found him stretched out on the sofa. Sitting up, scratching, he said hello to the man who was coming through the doorway behind her, who then declined coffee after all and left quickly. To the departing back of this man who was old enough to be Monica's father, Stanley said loudly, 'I suppose he has to get home to his wife and kids.'

Now Stanley, reclining, putting his shoes on the hotel's sofa, says to Monica, 'Does Michael know about you and his dad?'

Monica is taken aback. She had no idea Stanley knew the man he saw coming out of her room that morning. Stanley, clearly enjoying her discomfort, keeps her waiting before explaining, 'I used to get private tuition from Mr Porter when I was a kid. I went to his house so I always saw his kids too – Michael and his brothers and sisters. There were always loads of kids there. I always imagined I could just sort of stay and no one would notice. But of course I was always sent home.'

'His dad and me, that was years ago,' says Monica. 'I didn't know Michael then.'

'Did you get crabs?'

'What?'

'Did Mr Porter give you crabs?'

She stares at him.

'He always had crabs,' says Stanley.

She feels as if she is, at this very moment, crawling with lice.

'I have to get back to Michael,' she says, standing, returning her magazine to the table. Stanley reaches over and picks it up, settling down to read what she was reading, without saying goodbye.

She finds Michael asleep. She also finds that she has left the dental kit downstairs and has to get into bed without brushing her teeth. She sleeps badly and is already up when the wake-up call disturbs Michael. 'How's your mange?' he says, which makes her scratch.

They walk down to breakfast and Michael says, 'You're on edge. Antihistamines can do that to you.'

Monica doesn't have much of an appetite but Michael makes the most of the buffet, eating as if he might never eat again, as if he will not be facing an airline lunch in a few hours.

Afterwards, he goes to pay his mini-bar bill while Monica goes back to their room to collect their things.

She is straightening their bedding when she hears someone knocking on the door. Opening it, she finds Stanley outside. He is holding out the toothbrush she left behind last night. 'I used your toothbrush,' he says. 'You don't mind, do you? I've nothing catching.' Peering past her, he says, 'Nice room. It's bigger than mine. But then mine's a single.'

'I was about to leave,' says Monica.

'I saw Michael at the front desk, settling his bill.'

Monica stiffens, although she is relieved to think that this must be how he knows her room number; that he has not been in an adjacent bedroom, on the other side of a thin wall.

'He didn't remember me,' says Stanley.

His mouth, no longer hidden by facial hair, is quite unpleasant, thinks Monica. He never quite closes it.

He looks suddenly pained. He puts his hand on his crotch. 'I have to piss,' he says. Monica finds herself stepping aside so that Stanley can come in. He pushes open the bathroom door and then closes it behind him.

Monica shoulders her bag. She waits, hearing nothing through the bathroom door.

By the time he comes out, she has put the bag down again. It is heavy and the strap – a detachable leather one – digs into her shoulder. Preparing to leave, she picks her bag up again. Stanley, still zipping his fly, goes to the bed and sits down.

'I've been made redundant,' he says. 'I'm blowing my severance pay on two weeks in the Caribbean.'

'I want to go downstairs,' she says.

'Do you find yourself,' he asks, 'at our age, seeking out the people you knew when you were younger?' Looking down between his legs, he says, 'Your bedspread's the same as mine, Monica.'

It occurs to her that she could just go, leaving him here. Taking one last look around the room, she says, 'You can let yourself out.'

'Don't you want to know,' says Stanley, as Monica is walking to the door, 'what Michael and I talked about?'

Monica pauses with her back to him, frozen like someone with a gun pointed at her, the sight trained on the back of her head. 'Not especially,' she says.

'I told him how I know you,' he says, 'told him some stories about the good old days.' He lies down, putting his head on Monica's pillow, the soles of his shoes on the bedspread. He closes his eyes. 'I didn't mention Mr Porter senior.'

'I'm going,' she says.

'I need to piss again,' moans Stanley. 'Or I feel like I do. I've got some kind of infection. I keep wanting to piss but nothing comes out. It just hurts.' He scampers to the bathroom and as he shuts himself in he says, 'I suppose we'll see one another on the plane. We should meet up in Barbados, go for a drink, tell Michael some more of our stories.'

Monica stands for a moment outside the closed door. Slowly, she slips the bag off her shoulder and unclips the wide leather strap. Quietly fastening one end around the bathroom door handle, she pulls the strap taut and loops it around the handle of an adjacent cupboard, wrapping it around both handles a couple more times before securing it, with difficulty because her hands are shaking.

Picking up her bag again, she leaves the room, hanging the 'do not disturb' sign on the door handle. She looks at her watch. She should be on the plane by the time the maid discovers him.

She has to stop herself hurrying down the stairs, rushing into the lobby. She finds Michael sitting in the lounge area, on the sofa where Stanley sat the night before.

'We should get going,' says Monica, 'if we don't want to miss the plane.'

'The bus won't be here yet,' says Michael, but Monica is already heading for the exit. Michael follows her. They have just got outside when he says, 'Oh, I left my book in the bathroom. Did you pick it up?' When Monica hesitates, he says, 'I'll nip up and get it. I'll get the key back from reception.'

'I've got your book,' says Monica, peering down the empty road. 'It's in my bag.'

'I can read the last chapter on the plane,' says Michael. 'Oh, I met someone called Stanley. He said he was a friend of yours. You shared a house or something.'

'Not really,' she says.

She keeps glancing at the hotel entrance, and Michael, noticing, eyeing her goosepimples, says, 'Do you want to wait inside? Are you cold?'

'No,' she says, 'I just want to get going.'

'Me too,' says Michael. 'I want to be on the plane.'

Monica says nothing. She looks up at the overcast sky.

From her seat near the back of the bus, Monica watches the door, flinching at every thin body glimpsed through the window, every bald head ducking on entering.

'Are you looking for your friend?' asks Michael. 'Is he supposed to be on this bus?'

'He's not really my friend,' says Monica.

Even when people stop boarding, the bus waits. Eventually, the engine is switched on. The bus idles, spewing fumes, before slowly pulling away from the kerb, and Monica relaxes into her seat.

She pictures Stanley sitting in the bathroom, reading Michael's blockbuster. She knows she has only delayed him, and that when he is found, he will just take another flight, but Barbados is big enough, although she will no doubt find herself looking over her shoulder, never feeling quite at ease, preferring to stay in the hotel. Their paths won't cross on the return journey because Stanley will go home after two weeks but they are staying for three. And he doesn't know where they live. With any luck, she will never see him again.

They head for the airport, picking up speed.

It is raining as they cross the tarmac. They hurry towards the plane, running for cover as if the raindrops were a hail of bullets.

They climb the metal staircase. At the top, a stewardess greets them warmly without making eye contact. The cabin smells peachy. They have sprayed something, thinks Monica, to mask the smell of sick.

They slip into their seats and fasten their seatbelts. Monica turns to the rain-spattered window, peering anxiously out. Michael says, 'You're like the man in *The Twilight Zone* who sees a gremlin on the wing of the plane. Are you worried?'

Beta blockers, thinks Monica. She would like beta blockers to numb her to this, the awfulness of this flight.

'I'll be all right,' she says, 'once we're in the air.'

Passengers continue to board and she watches their unhurried search for their seats, their dithering over what to put in the lockers, the aisles clogging.

Michael inspects the contents of the pocket on the back of the seat in front – laminated emergency instructions, cartoons of people dealing calmly with disaster, and an in-flight magazine through which he leafs, browsing photographs of other destinations they might have chosen.

Monica watches another plane taxiing down the wet runway. The backs of her legs are itching against the seat fabric. She is hours away from her next tablet.

Michael reaches for Monica's bag and hunts through it. 'Where's my book?' he says.

Monica goes through the motions of looking through the bag herself. 'I don't think it's here.'

'You said you'd picked it up.'

'I thought I did.' She is still searching, although pointlessly, there being barely anything in the bag to hunt through. She doesn't turn to look at him, knowing that if she does she will find him looking at her as if she is crazy. In the end, she shrugs and apologises. She takes out the magazine she has bought and yesterday's bottle of water. As she unscrews the lid and lifts the bottle to her mouth, her hand is shaking.

Michael sighs. 'We should be going soon,' he says. He looks at his watch. 'We should have gone already.' Monica opens her magazine to a centre spread of women with circles around the sweat patches under their arms.

There is a disturbance towards the front of the plane and she looks up to see the faltering smile of the stewardess at the door, and Michael says, 'Is that your friend?'

Glory Hole

IN THE SMALL hours, Peter wakes. He listens, wondering if his wife is in her bed yet or if she is still downstairs. On other nights, he has heard her laughing and has thought to himself that she never laughed like that before her brother arrived; or he has heard the guitar music the brother plays with his long fingernails; or he has been woken by the sound of the brother pissing like a racehorse in the bathroom.

The brother turned up with a guitar and an overnight bag more than a month ago. They used to have a spare room but Peter's wife sleeps in there now so they put her brother in the lounge. It smells of him, of his unmade bed, his unwashed clothes.

Every evening, after dinner in the kitchen, Peter excuses himself from the table, leaving the two of them talking. The brother does not speak English. Neither did Peter's wife when he first met her, in the canteen of the local college where she was taking a beginners' class. She was attractive, friendly, keen, but there were months of canteen coffee and dates before they went back to her flat. He remembers her bedroom, her overwhelming perfume, her straddling him, seeming huge above him in the dark room. He did not know where to put his hands and wondered afterwards whether he had touched her at all.

Peter doesn't understand a word they say, but if he asks his wife what they talk about she tells him.

❧

'You have holes in the walls of your public toilets.'

'Holes?'

'So that two people can have sex without seeing one another.'

'Oh.'

'A man can put himself through a hole and receive sex. But he doesn't know who is on the other side. He hopes it is someone who will give him pleasure.'

Peter is always the first to go to bed and the first to get up in the morning. He potters about in the kitchen for hours until the brother appears wearing his bed sheet like a toga, greeting Peter with a warm hand on the back of his neck, or on the curve where his neck meets his shoulder, squeezing slightly, and Peter feels those long fingernails digging into his skin.

Peter is thinking of saying to his wife that maybe it's time her brother was moving on.

'You also have holes between the booths in your adult video stores.'

'I don't know.'

'Yes, you do. If you want to do something to the other man, you put your finger through the hole.'

'Your finger?'

'That's how you invite him to put himself through. If he does, you can do something to him.'

Peter's evening class was in creative writing, but he did not complete the course. His characters – who always seemed to be waiting for something, for a train, a phone call, a knock at the door, and to whom something was inevitably going to happen – made him anxious. He left these stories unfinished and hasn't written since, although he has been thinking about trying again.

Someone is coming up the stairs. Peter could just stay where he is, warm in his bed, but he is getting out, slowly crossing the room in the dark, hesitating for a moment before opening the door.

Reaching the top of the stairs, turning to look when Peter's bedroom door opens, is the brother. He is naked, scratching himself with those long fingernails which Peter feels on the back of his neck every morning, which he feels digging into his skin, even now.

Nurture

EVERY DAY, MARK swims a mile of front crawl. He swallows a lot of swimming pool water and gets out with chlorine in his gut, his bladder bursting. There used to be disinfectant to paddle through on the way to the changing room, but that has gone. He takes a hot shower before heading home.

As a child, he took himself to the pool on Saturday mornings, leaving his mum and dad and sister on the sofa in front of the TV. By the time he got back, his dad was starting in the garden. Even now, the smell of chlorine brings to mind his dad standing in the middle of his imperfect lawn holding a spray gun full of weedkiller.

Under the grass, there were dozens of bulbs, and every spring, the green shoots pushed through. Mark's dad glared at the unwelcome buds which ravaged his lawn. They were pests, like the slugs which ruined the marigolds, and the maggots which bred in the vegetable patch. He kept on digging them out, and they kept on coming up. Mark's mum said could he not just leave them be?

The bulbs had been planted before they lived there. Mark's mum and dad and sister had lived somewhere else before Mark was born. It seemed to Mark that they had been happier in this other place than they were now, and he wondered why they didn't still live there, why they couldn't go back; he would have liked to live there too.

He begged his mum to take him there, to see this house in which he did not exist, where they lived their lives without him. In the end, she took him. They went on a bus whose windows looked as if they had not been washed or even rained on in weeks, and the world Mark saw through them seemed dirty.

They got off at a bus shelter whose glass had been smashed. They walked the few metres to the mouth of a dingy alleyway where his mum stopped. 'I don't want to,' she said, holding on to a street sign as if someone were going to make her. She stood, grim-faced, staring into the alleyway as if there were something dreadful down there, amid the stink of bins, even though Mark could see nothing but shadows.

She turned away, returning them to the bus stop to wait for another grimy bus which would take them back to where they had got on.

Walking home from their stop, it seemed like it might rain soon, and Mark's mum hurried them along, looking anxiously at the sky, at the clouds' swollen underbellies, not wanting to get caught in a downpour.

'Don't tell your dad we went there,' she said, and Mark promised, even though he thought that surely they hadn't been there after all.

Sometimes his dad, objecting to Mark's language or to a look, snatched him up by his collar, gathering shirt and skin and hair in his fist, and carried him out into the garden. Then Mark, feeling like an animal picked up and dropped by a tornado, was deposited into the flowerbed. He felt his dad's big, warm hand on the back of his neck, pushing him down until the turned soil pressed against his mouth, getting in between his lips and into his nostrils. Grit crunched between his teeth. He tasted the dirt on his tongue, felt it in his throat, felt all the things which crawled in it crawling in him, crawling and shitting and breeding in him.

They went on holiday one summer to a converted barn on a French farm. Mark found ants living under the porch and was playing with them when the farmer's big boots stopped beside him. Mark looked up. The farmer, whose smell reminded Mark of the beer in which his dad drowned slugs, said something, but in French, and Mark did not understand. The farmer gestured: *Come with me.*

Mark followed the farmer across the yard and into a corrugated-iron cow shed which smelt of metal and piss and warm animal breath. At the far end of the shed, they stopped and the farmer nodded towards a dim corner. Mark saw a dog in the damp and stinking straw, straining, its body trembling, a bitch with something between her legs, something slipping wetly out of her. He heard mewling.

He showed his sister the puppies in the cow shed and the ants under the house. They gave the ants some sugar and watched them carry it away.

One morning, when the others went out walking, Mark stayed behind in the house. It was a warm day. He had the back door wide open for the breeze and was getting himself a cold drink from the fridge when he heard whimpering behind him. Turning, he saw a dog in the doorway, one of the farm dogs standing just inside the kitchen, dripping blood. Mark narrowed his eyes. He shut the fridge and opened a drawer. Approaching the dog, he raised his arm and brought a wooden rolling pin down hard on the dog's black nose. He banged it down again and then again until the dog finally dropped the savaged puppy from between its jaws. Mark released the rolling pin and crouched down, bending over the small, ruined body. He moved to touch it and the dog snapped its empty and blood-wet jaws around his hand, its teeth breaking the skin, sinking into the flesh.

Mark did not hear himself shouting, but he supposed that he must have done, that between them they must have made enough noise to bring the farmer's wife running.

The farmer's wife tied the dog up outside and inspected Mark's wounds. She did not seem surprised by the sight of the puppy lying on the floor; she just seemed disappointed.

She spoke to Mark in English and he asked her why the dog had done that to its puppy. 'That's not one of his,' she said, and Mark thought about nature programmes he'd seen in which dominant lions kill the young which aren't theirs.

The farmer's wife went for a first-aid kit and while she was gone Mark's parents and sister returned from their walk. Mark met them in the hallway and told them what had happened.

'Jesus,' said his mum, seeing the blood leaking from him, dripping from his fingertips. 'Get off the carpet.' She steered him back into the kitchen. The puppy was still there but she did not look at it. Fetching a cloth from the sink, she returned to the hallway and tried to clean the blood off the carpet but a stain remained. She moved the doormat to cover it, and meanwhile Mark's dad was boiling water to pour under the porch.

The dog bite healed, with Mark doing his best not to pick at the scabs. When they came away, they left behind patches of new pink skin which were not quite smooth to the touch.

Mark's voice deepened. Dark hairs sprouted on his weak chin. He grew tall, filling doorways, startling his mum on the landing.

His teachers talked to him about his falling grades. He was warned about antisocial behaviour, and then suspended. Mark took his exams but was not encouraged to stay on for the sixth form.

Abroad again that summer, they stayed in a hotel with a pool and sun loungers on which they lay in their swimwear, Mark dripping wet from the lengths he swam, his sister dozing in a bikini, his mum with a beach towel wrapped around her, her eyes closed although she was awake, swatting at invisible insects. His dad sat upright in a plastic chair, his eyes open. Mark's mum suddenly said brightly, looking at her grown-up daughter and her school-leaver son, 'I suppose this could be our last ever holiday together.'

Mark got an interview for a job with the council and his mum ironed a shirt for him to wear. His dad, finding him waiting bare-chested in the living room doorway, said Mark ought to be ironing his own shirt, not standing there watching her do it.

'Leave him be,' said his mum. 'It's only a shirt.'

'If you get this job,' she said to Mark, finishing the shirt and holding it out to him, 'you could get a place of your own.'

When Mark returned from his interview, he found his mum still ironing. She ironed everything, even underwear and sheets. His dad was in his armchair, reading the paper. Mark, shrugging off his jacket as he came into the living room, said, 'I got it.'

'Oh good,' said his mum with relief. 'That's really good.' She put down the iron and held out a hand, perhaps for his jacket, while Mark, coming towards her, responded with an awkward hug, feeling her stiffen.

'I thought I'd fucked it up,' he said, pulling away again, his mum turning to her ironing pile. Going on to explain about 'a bastard of a question' he'd been asked, he felt his dad's hand at the back of his neck, going for his collar. Mark swung around and pushed his dad away, shoving him backwards into the ironing board. His dad, as he lost his balance, snatched at Mark's shirt, whose little white buttons scattered around them like seeds being sown. His mum steadied the ironing board, but his dad, falling, trying to hold on to something, grabbed the iron's cord and brought the burning-hot, three-pound appliance down on his head. On the floor, holding a hand to his wound, to the place where it hurt, he said to Mark's mum, 'You should have had it aborted.'

Mark's sister, looking out of the window, puts on a raincoat. Her mum, going with her to the door, says, 'Give him my love.' Her dad is sitting in his chair, staring at the TV, at some old programme. He says nothing.

She takes a bus to the park and then walks between waterlogged flowerbeds to the pond. She finds Mark waiting on a damp bench. He smells of chlorine. In one hand he is holding a bag of bread for the ducks. His other hand is empty and she can see the pattern in his skin, a join-the-dots puzzle of pale blemishes in the shape of a smile, the shape of a jaw. Sitting down on that side, she reaches for his hand. Telling him, 'Mum sends her love,' she touches his scars.

Seclusion

MAUREEN, COMING OUT of her back bedroom, closing the door behind her, hears a noise. She stands in the hallway, in the middle of her bungalow, listening, trying to work out where it is coming from, this sound which is a bit like birds scrabbling inside the walls, mice scratching in the loft.

She remembers Jane saying that the police would come round and check the house for weak points, potential entry points, but Maureen thinks she was supposed to arrange this herself – the Neighbourhood Watch leaflet has a number to call – and she hasn't. Maureen has double glazing throughout now and keeps her windows closed, and she knows she has bolted the front door but the side door might have been left unlocked. She steps from the hallway into the kitchen but sees nothing there, no one at the door, no one at the windows, and the noise has stopped.

She knows Jane worries about her living alone. Maureen does not have any close neighbours to keep an eye on her. If she did not make a point of getting herself out to the shops and to the library for large-print books, and to Jane's on Sundays, it would be possible to go for weeks without seeing anyone.

Jane lives nearby in a one-bedroom flat which she rarely leaves. She is, thinks Maureen, getting worse. Jane did go to university but soon came back. She tried an office job or two before finding something that she could do from home. She has never been abroad – she does not have a passport. She tried Glastonbury once and Maureen worried dreadfully about her, about strangers and crowds, although sometimes one is safer with plenty of people around. Either way, Jane came home sunburnt but otherwise unharmed, although she did not go again. Jane has to be careful in the sun because of her colouring, which, Maureen has told her, comes from Eddie, whom Jane has never met.

Eddie was unlike the others, who tended to remove their wedding rings before sitting down next to Maureen and offering to buy her a drink. Eddie kept his wedding ring on even when he was in Maureen's bed. And while most of the men, in the end, talked about nothing but their wives and marriages, Eddie only mentioned his wife to say to Maureen, 'I won't leave her, you know.' This was, thought Maureen, probably because of the baby she sometimes saw sleeping in a pram in Eddie's front garden.

Maureen fantasised about being married to Eddie. She imagined contented evenings spent together in front of the television, him with the top button of his trousers undone after a big dinner which she had cooked, and her dandling their baby.

When she told him – as he was driving her home – that she was pregnant, he said nothing until he drew up outside the flat she shared with another girl. She got out of the car and then he said, 'You can't have it.'

She did not see much of him after that. He stopped calling. When she went to his house, no one came to the door, until finally his wife answered and told her to stop bothering him.

Eddie was a bus conductor but Maureen did not know his routes. In the end, she waited outside the depot until he came out. He was wearing his uniform, with a peaked cap. He did not blank her, as she had worried he might, but he looked beyond her while they talked. She said she missed him. He told her he'd been busy, that he was doing extra shifts because his wife was expecting again. Anyway, he said, it was time he was getting home, and he went on his way without having looked once at the huge pram between them, without even glancing at the baby inside, a girl. Maureen would have preferred a boy.

She knew, as Eddie walked away, that she would have to leave now, put some distance between herself and this small town.

A hundred miles away, she met and moved in with Frank. He was a wonderful father to Jane, changing sodden and long-soiled nappies and remembering feeds when Maureen did not. He was attentive but not a worrier, whereas Maureen was forgetful but anxious. Frank thought that Maureen was over-protective. He objected to Jane being kept indoors most of the time as if she were one of Maureen's shade-loving plants, and he did not agree with Jane being home-schooled. He said Jane was sheltered, as if this were a bad thing. Maureen kept her safe, unlike some mothers.

Frank knew about Eddie and had always expected him to come looking for Maureen, wanting to see Jane. 'He won't come,' said Maureen, although a part of her always thought he might appear on her doorstep one day. She would not let him in.

※

Back in the hallway, she sees, through the porthole window in the UPVC front door, a dark shape, a man's head. Jane said, 'Keep your hallway light on, to show prowlers there's somebody in.' But Maureen has switched the lights off, and the radio.

She had them on – the hallway light and the kitchen light and Radio 2 – at dawn this morning. She wakes early these days despite her sleeping pills, and cannot get off again. Sometimes she wakes in the middle of the night, hearing things – those little sounds which she can put down to mice or the pipes or the wind, and the not-so-little noises of the boys who bring their motorbikes up here, and people having sex against her front wall. She has tried to talk to the council about it; she has written letters, but nothing has been done. If it gets to be too much, she turns her hearing aid down.

Opening the fridge and looking for milk for her porridge, she found that she was almost out. She put on her coat and left the house, and the streetlights were still on as she headed down the hill towards a supermarket which would be open even at that hour. She did not expect to see many people. At the bottom of the hill, she entered an alleyway. This took her to the main road, which she crossed, entering another alleyway which forked. The fork she took would bring her out just around the corner from the supermarket.

In the alleyway, she passed a man out walking his dog. She said, 'Good morning,' but only the dog looked at her. Another man, drunk, chatted away, but only to himself. Perhaps he saw her, but he would not remember her. Maureen, who used to turn heads, these days goes unnoticed, unheard, untouched. She feels like a wife in the soundproof booth on Mr & Mrs.

As she emerged from the alleyway, she saw a young woman sitting on a bench in front of an empty office block. Beside her was a pram, and Maureen stopped to look inside it. Seeing a lovely baby boy, she tried to pay the mother a compliment but the young woman was wearing headphones and did not hear her, paid her no attention.

Maureen went on past the office block and into the supermarket. In the doorway, she passed a security guard who reminded her of Eddie, his red hair curling out from beneath his peaked cap, his gaze elsewhere.

She took a bottle of milk from the fridge and made her way back towards the checkout, pausing at the cosmetics to look at a lipstick in a shade called 'tea rose pink'. It would go nicely, she thought, with a dress she might wear if Donald came round for dinner.

She has been on her own for a few years now and Jane has been nagging her about finding someone. 'You need a man about the house,' she keeps saying. Maureen met Donald at the library. He gave her one of his Neighbourhood Watch leaflets and invited her to a meeting. She said she could not go but he took her number anyway. They have spoken on the phone a few times since then. He likes gardening, Radio 4, a good dinner. She is expecting him to call.

Having paid for her milk at the self-service checkout, she left the shop. The security guard who looked like Eddie had gone. The young woman was there though, still on the bench with the baby in the pram beside her.

Maureen sees the brush now, scrubbing at the little round window in the door. There is a trickle of water coming in underneath, darkening the edge of the mat. Window cleaners, appearing suddenly at her windows, make her nervous. The old one used to come to the door with his bucket, asking for clean water, but this one is self-contained, carrying gallons in his van. He will knock, wanting money, but she will not open the door.

She returns to the back bedroom. It used to be Jane's room. Now Maureen keeps her shade-loving plants – a begonia and a philodendron – in there. The room gets no direct sunlight and the plants are on a shelf far away from the window but still they are failing to thrive. Maureen closes the curtains.

There is a bucket underneath a leak in the ceiling. By the time she remembers to empty it, though, it is usually overflowing. There is an old armchair in one corner in which she used to sit and bottle-feed Jane and in which she still occasionally takes a nap. Jane took her single bed with her, and other bits of furniture and the posters from the walls, leaving the room rather empty.

Maureen has kept, up in the loft, Jane's old cot, and cardboard boxes full of baby things, thinking that they would be needed when Jane had children, but that's unlikely now, at Jane's age. Maureen has offered many times to look after the baby if Jane had one, has said how nice it would be to have another child in the house.

She can hear the window cleaner knocking on the front door. She waits in the darkened back bedroom until he gives up. After a minute, she hears him leaving in his van.

Maureen goes to the kitchen and puts a pan on the hob. Opening the fridge, she takes out the almost empty bottle of skimmed milk and pours the last of it into the pan. She lights the hob underneath it and looks around for the milk she bought at the shop but she can't see it anywhere.

The phone rings. It is unlikely to be Jane, who does not like telephones. Maureen lets the answering machine take a message. It is Donald, accepting her invitation to dinner, asking what time, needing to know her address. She does not want him to come now, does not want him in her house, clomping through her rooms, poking around, wanting to see the begonia, the philodendron. She waits for his call to end and then deletes the message. She puts her hand in her pocket, takes out the pink lipstick and drops it into the bin.

She hears the hiss of the milk pan boiling dry. Removing the pan from the hob and taking it to the sink, she notices the cat's empty bowl. She cannot recall when she last saw the cat. She has not put any food down for days. She goes to fetch a tin from the cupboard but there is nothing in there. She is sure she had some. Things go missing. She has no idea where they end up. Her clothes pegs have wandered, and she used to have more teaspoons.

A bowl of milk might bring the cat in but she cannot remember what she has done with the new bottle.

She left the shop with the bottle in her hand, the refrigerator chill in her fingers. It was almost too cold to carry. The young woman on the bench had her eyes closed. Her head was drooping despite whatever she was listening to through her headphones, noise which Maureen could faintly hear.

Behind the young woman, the empty office block's mirrored frontage reflected the rising sun. It looked so much like a building on fire that Maureen almost expected to hear an alarm, sirens in the distance, but there was nothing. She paused again to look into the pram, to see the baby dozing beneath the silently blazing windows, and then, without disturbing either of them, went quietly into the alleyway.

The one thing Maureen has not kept is Jane's pram. It was so big and heavy. She approves of the smaller and lighter modern pram, more easily manoeuvred through the alleyways and up the hill and through the front door which she remembered to lock behind her.

She goes once more into the shade of the back bedroom. Reaching into the pram, she fetches out the milk. The baby's blanket is cold where the bottle has been resting.

Maureen returns to the kitchen, where the phone is ringing again.

She locks the side door.

Sleeping Under the Stars

FROM THE SPARE room window, I can see into the back gardens, as far as number twenty, where men are laying new turf.

We, at number two, sometimes used to get number twenty's letters and it was my job to take them round. Mr Batten's house was pretty much the same as ours. If you looked, you could see the differences, but when I stood on the doorstep and knocked, it felt like knocking at my own back door, and when Mr Batten answered, it was like there was a strange man standing in our kitchen while I stood outside looking in.

Mr Batten lived alone. He had rabbits, and a grown-up daughter who no longer visited.

At the far end of the street, there is a corner shop, to which my mother sends me for the ingredients she finds she is missing in the middle of baking. I started stopping off at Mr Batten's to see his rabbits. He always had sweets – fat coils of black liquorice, and chocolate limes with hard, sour shells and softly oozing insides.

He was always there. And then, one day, he wasn't.

It was the kind of autumn day when the day before had seemed like summer but suddenly you could feel winter coming – there was condensation on the windows – and I, still in a T-shirt, was unprepared.

In the shop, two women stood near the fridge, talking in low voices while I browsed the dairy products. Seeing me, they went quiet, and they looked like the words trapped behind their sealed lips were something horrid and squirmy, like worms wriggling on their tongues. The fridge hummed and my bare arms goosepimpled.

I walked home past number twenty but on the other side of the road. I gave my mother the shopping and she made pastry. I watched her rolling it flat and laying it smoothly over the top of her pie dish and removing the untidy edges with a knife.

I never saw Mr Batten again.

I once took my best friend Donna into the spare room to watch television, forgetting about the unmade sofa bed and the pyjamas on the floor.

'Who's sleeping in here?' she asked.

'My dad,' I said.

The spare room is where visitors sleep, but sometimes my dad does too. His pillows and a blanket appear on the sofa bed and stay there for a few days, and then they disappear, and sometimes my dad does too.

'Why is he sleeping in here?' asked Donna.

'I don't know,' I said, switching on the television, a portable on top of a desk.

'Have you got any DVDs?' she asked.

'No,' I said, 'I don't think so.'

'What's in here?' She was trying to open the desk drawer. 'Why's it locked?'

'I don't know.'

Taking a kirby grip out of her hair, she said, 'I can pick a lock.'

'Don't,' I said. 'That's my dad's stuff.'

But she already had the grip in the drawer's tiny keyhole.

She was poking it around, saying, 'Let's see what he's got,' and then the drawer opened. She rifled through the contents, clearly disappointed. 'It's just birthday cards,' she said, 'and Father's Day cards. There's a photo of you.' She held it out, a picture of a little girl wearing a paper hat on her head and sitting on her dad's lap.

'Put it back,' I said.

Donna put the photo away again and closed the drawer. She fixed the kirby grip into her hair and we watched something on the television, I forget what.

My mother kept our photos in albums. I liked to sit and look at them, especially the ones of me when I was small – me and my dad at Christmas, me and my dad on my birthday. I looked at the photos so often it was as if I could remember these things happening, as if I knew how it felt to sit on his lap that Christmas when I was just a baby – my fingers exploring his watch and his wrist, his ring and his knuckles, his valuables and his bones – even though I couldn't possibly have done.

My mother is downstairs making Stargazy pie, and I have a bag of liquorice laces from the shop. I have one in my mouth; it curls wetly on my tongue while I watch the men at work at number twenty. I wish I had bought sherbet flying saucers instead.

That autumn, soon after the day when I heard the women talking by the fridge, I was sent to Grandma's even though it was term time. Before I left, a tent the colour of uncooked pastry appeared behind Mr Batten's house. People went into the tent, and things came out.

I once slept in a tent in our back garden. The tent was

a present for my birthday which is in September, and even though it wasn't summer any more I was allowed to spend the night camping on the lawn with Donna. The air was fresh, as if we were lying out in the open, except that we couldn't see the stars. 'Sleeping under the stars,' my dad called it, but all we could see was the roof of the tent.

We lay on our backs, looking up, and Donna said, 'Did you know there are thousands of worms in your garden? They surface at night.' And she said, 'Did you know there are a million bits of man-made junk orbiting the Earth?' It was zooming around, she said, at twenty-five thousand miles per hour, disintegrating silently in space or dropping into Earth's atmosphere and bulleting towards the ground.

Donna wanted to be able to see the night sky, to see the abandoned satellites and bits of jettisoned spacecraft hurtling towards us, but I preferred to sleep beneath the polyester roof of my little tent, where I couldn't see the sky falling. I pulled my sleeping bag up to my neck and closed my eyes. I lay in the dark with autumn's musty smells – damp leaves rotting and cold earth – in my nostrils, and the chill of the ground against my body, trying not to think about all the worms squirming up beneath me, trying not to think about the space graveyard.

It was the same cold – autumn cold, outdoor cold, damp cold – at Grandma's. She did not believe in central heating, she believed in jumpers and hot drinks. Sleeping in my mother's old bedroom, I imagined her, in childhood, lying between these same cold sheets, in this same darkness and silence, and it felt almost as if we were one and the same child who had been lying there since the 1970s.

We had bran for breakfast. It sat brown and heavy in my

stomach while Grandma and I finished her crossword and played Scrabble and did wordsearches, and she said, 'I'm a bit of a word worm, my dear.'

We looked at her photo albums. She had a copy of a picture we had at home, of that Christmas when I was a baby, sitting on my dad's knee.

'That's not your dad,' said Grandma. 'That's your Uncle John.'

They were twins, my dad and Uncle John. They were so alike – you had to look closely to spot the difference. I stared at the picture of the man who held me on his lap, looking at the style of his hair and the easiness of his smile, seeing the silver signet ring on his right hand and the bare ring finger on his left.

Grandma made Stargazy pie. But where my mother's had a smooth lid of pastry, Grandma's had a dozen fish heads poking out, their bodies buried beneath the crust – pilchards with gaping mouths and glazed eyes staring up at the ceiling.

'What your mother makes,' she said, 'is not Stargazy pie. This is Stargazy pie. What your mother makes is just fish pie.'

I sat down, trying not to look at it.

'I made this for you when you were little,' she said, 'when I came to stay.' She cut into the crust and shovelled a piece of this alarming meal onto my plate, fish heads and all. 'You can't eat the heads,' she said. 'Leave them on the side.' She put some pie in her mouth and when she had chewed and swallowed it she added, 'When your father left.'

I removed my fish heads and pushed them to the side of my plate, trying to see only the fish pie remaining, like my mother made.

'Your mother never liked looking at the heads,' she said. 'Or didn't like them looking at her.' She filled her mouth again and when she was ready she said, 'There was another woman, you see. Your first Christmas, he was with her.' She glared at the fish heads sitting in her pie, as if she too, after all, found them distasteful. The mouths of the disembodied fish heads on my plate hung silently open. 'They weren't married, your father and this woman, but they had a child; he had another family. He came back, and then left again when you were two or three. That's when I came to stay with you. I made you my Stargazy pie and you liked it.' In the dimming kitchen, Grandma's voice bored softly through me. 'You have a half-sister,' she said. 'Your mother won't tell you that, and nor will your father, but I think you should know.'

When I looked at the fish heads I could almost feel their slithery skin on my tongue. Grandma watched me until I took a forkful of pie and put it in my mouth.

'Of course you don't remember,' she said. 'You were too little. And of course she took him back again.'

She carved out her fish heads and put them aside and ate what was left.

Chewing, I felt a milk tooth shift, and the sickening looseness in my jaw was like subsidence in my mouth.

My liquorice laces taste nasty, but even so I can't stop eating them. There is a slimy mass of them in my mouth, waiting to slide down into my queasy stomach.

When I went to stay with Grandma, my summer clothes were still to hand. When I returned, it was the middle of winter. The leaves had fallen from the trees, exposing the bare, bony branches. The houses looked dingy in the winter light, like greyed teeth.

Mr Batten's house was pulled down. They used a digger which made the whole street shudder. Strangers came wanting bits of the rubble, bits of that broken house to keep as souvenirs, trophy hunting. When I asked my mother why, she said, 'People do strange things.'

There are pillows and a blanket on the sofa bed. I know the desk drawer will be locked, although I haven't tried it. I know how to pick the lock now, but I don't do it. There is a photograph in there which I don't want to see – the picture Donna found of a little girl sitting on my dad's lap, a paper hat on her head; a little girl who could have been me, but wasn't.

At number twenty, in the space where Mr Batten used to live, the turf is being unrolled like a new carpet over the dirt. It will be a garden and people will be quiet there.

I go down to the kitchen and watch my mother draping pastry over her pie, trimming the surplus, her knife scraping around the rim of the dish, and my tongue keeps straying to the strange gaps where my milk teeth used to be.

Jetsam

'Most of our DNA is actually obsolete . . . composed largely of sequences for dead genes – for the fins we once had, for webbed feet, for a tail that had thrashed.

'Three hundred millennia on, our blood is mainly, stubbornly, salt water.'

ALISON MACLEOD, 'Pilot'

B ESIDE A CRUMBLING cliff path, an old house faces the creeping sea. An upstairs window has been opened a crack, and a breeze enters, shifting the heavy curtains and stirring the musty air. Daylight penetrates, illuminating treasure and junk and teeth and bone.

Down the corridor, the sunless back bedroom has space rocket wallpaper and 'JULES VERNE'S EVER POPULAR BOOKS FOR BOYS' on dusty shelves.

Downstairs, the kitchen radio has been left on. The breakfast things are still out. There is a china cup on the table, used by the nameless dead. There is sand in the butter and driftwood in the sink.

The rising tide approaches the cliffs.

He is in a stifling classroom, pushing at the painted-shut windows. There are fingermarks on the warm panes and in the sun-softened putty. His skin feels grubby in the heat. His tired eyes, blinking behind thick lenses, feel gritty in the dry air.

He has his back to his students, who yawn when he talks about the demise of the Phoenicians, the Sea People; they are bored by the collapse of empires. They could not care less about the ancient art which he holds in his hands, these faded fragments of another world. A bead of sweat runs down to the corner of his mouth and he tastes its salt.

On his way home, he stops at a second-hand bookshop. On a shelf near the back, he finds Victorian pornography – photographs of pale women, naked except for their hats and laced-up boots, staring into the camera so that when he gazes at them, they, long gone now, gaze back. He puts the book back on the shelf but his hand lingers on the bare and disintegrating spine, the dust of old leather clinging to his fingertips. He leaves with a brown-paper bulge in his pocket.

He peers through the window of the deserted charity shop, squinting through his own reflection, eyeing the cast-offs. His mother used to bring his father's old clothes here – jackets whose arms were too short, shoes whose soles were wearing thin. His father, finding his things missing, would go down to the charity shop and fetch them back. She would find his wretched shoes in the hallway again, like something thrown into the sea and washed right back onto the beach, lying forlornly at her feet.

He moves on, towards the collapsing cliffs and home, pausing on the doorstep to sniff at the sea before going inside.

In the fusty hallway, he slips off his shoes. On the wall, there is a ship's clock and a family portrait of his ancestors in sepia. He comes from a long line of Cornish tin miners, who worked deep below sea level, in the cold, in the dark, in torchlight. The mines were always in danger of flooding, of being reclaimed by the water. His father was the first not to go into mining. The tin miners - and their language - have all but gone now.

He rinses the china cup and picks the sand out of the butter. Before supper, he takes a walk on the dunes, on this peninsula which is an ophiolite - he is walking on the ocean floor. The sand is dry and hot.

There are centuries-old skeletons in the dunes - the remains of sailors who washed ashore, lay unclaimed and were anonymously interred above the high-water mark.

When ships are wrecked, his mother said, mermaids claim the drowned sailors. The sailors become mermen. She touched his cheek with cool fingers and leant close to kiss him, smelling of sea salt. He imagined these shipwrecked sailors sinking down with hopeful smiles on their faces, anticipating dewy eyes and cool hands and the kiss of life. But what, he wondered, if the mermaids did not want them?

He was born here, pushed out of the womb with a residue of amniotic fluid in his lungs.

His father was an archaeologist, coming home with traces of ancient graves on the soles of his boots, and souvenirs in his pockets, Palaeolithic treasures: necklaces and bracelets, snail shells and ivory beads, teeth and bone. His father was interested in stone-age art and cave paintings - the handprints and fingermarks made by humans reaching out through the cave walls to the spirit realm; images of spirit animals, and part-human, part-animal figures depicting men in altered states of consciousness (experiencing weightlessness and bleeding from the nose) travelling to the spirit world.

He remembers his mother's exasperation at the prehistoric dirt his father walked into the house and into the carpet, the fragments of anonymous skeletons he left on the kitchen table, his absorption in his work and his squirming with excitement over dead things. He remembers her cursing the damp walls which crumbled in her hands, the damp nooks and crannies where the silverfish thrived, the beams salvaged from the seabed rotting in the ceiling, and the sand which just kept coming in.

He remembers her at bedtime, her weight shifting on the edge of his mattress. He remembers *Twenty Thousand Leagues Under the Sea*, in which Captain Nemo takes a walk on the seabed, through a submarine forest and submarine coalmines and the flooded remains of Atlantis; and *Round the Moon*, in which men travel with dogs to the lunar continent and finish up in the sea, and the illustrations were of scuba divers and submarines. He remembers the wounded dog: *'They had merely to drop him into space, in the same way that sailors drop a body into the sea . . .'* He remembers the rhythm of her reading and her breathing, her voice rising and falling, her chest rising and falling, and her reaching the end of the chapter and closing the book without marking the page, and in the morning she was gone. He remembers her cool touch, her cool kiss, and salt.

He was seven years old when the Russians launched a dog into space. Lying in bed at night, surrounded by space rockets and distant planets and desolate moons, he imagined those bewildered canine travellers: Satellite with his broken skull and Laika who could not come home.

His mother had left behind most of her things, amongst

them a record player, and singles which he played too slowly so that they sounded like a man singing love songs sadly underwater.

His father bought a television, on which they watched the first *Doctor Who*, and *Stingray*, and Jacques Cousteau documentaries.

Alongside his father's archaeology magazines, diving magazines appeared, one of which carried a transcript of Cousteau's 'Homo Aquaticus' speech predicting men with gills. He learnt about partial pressures; oxygen toxicity and nitrogen narcosis; the altered states of mind experienced at depth: trances and hallucinations, confusion – the diver thinking he is surfacing when in fact he is diving deeper – and stupor. The deep sea sounded awesome, a wonderful and terrible place, full of hazards with beautiful names, like exotic flowers: embolisms, emphysema, hypoxia and cyanosis.

He was fascinated by the equipment which his father kept in the shower room and in the cupboard under the stairs: the stiff wetsuit, the steel aqualung, the lead weights.

His milky wrists and ankles were inching out of his clothes, and his toes made holes in his socks, poking through, like something amphibian shedding old skin. His eyes bulged at the girls, who had also grown, and who had *wiles*, which made him think of physical appendages like tentacles, full of something sticky and poisonous.

He watched his father walking into the sea and swimming out until he disappeared beneath the surface of the water. Longing to follow him, he swam instead along the shore, and lay on the beach, burying himself, pushing his fingers into the sand, the bones deep and cold.

His father emerged with nose bleeds and loot, struggling up the beach with his tank and his souvenirs: shells and coins; brass portholes, clocks and bells; a china cup with a worn gilt rim – the spoils of shipwrecks, and jetsam (which sounded like a semiprecious stone – amethyst, topaz and jetsam). They went home with salt on their lips and in their hair, with sand between their teeth and their toes and under their fingernails, with the sea in their ears and their nostrils.

Frogmen found Atlantis, or the place where it had been, off the coast of Florida, and the Doctor found it south of the Azores, on the Mid-Atlantic Ridge. And spacemen landed on the moon, walking on the lunar surface as if they were walking underwater, with the sound of their own breathing in their ears.

There was a girl. They spent a lot of time lying on the dunes. This girl would always make him think of sand. They lay there at the start of a storm, gazing up at the inky darkness as the rain began to fall. He goosepimpled beneath her cold hands. She tasted of salt.

She left him, and once again he found himself alone at the edge of the sea, where dysphoria and chlamydia bloomed.

His father had begun to start sentences he couldn't finish, forgetting the beginning before reaching the end, stopping in the middle, an ellipsis floating from his lips like air bubbles underwater. On his way to the charity shop to fetch back clothes he had not had for years, his father hummed the love songs his wife had left behind, and when he returned, empty-handed, he went looking for her in the kitchen.

Meanwhile, the Russians were searching for Atlantis off the coast of Cornwall, and the British were looking for it at the bottom of a lake in Bolivia.

The light is going. The sand has cooled. The tide is coming in.

He always thought she would come back.

He walks home in the dusk, treading carefully, with skeletons beneath his feet and driftwood in his hands. He has a migraine coming on. He still has his father's old scuba equipment but his migraines bar him from diving.

He puts the driftwood into the kitchen sink. There is something on the radio about an ancient Middle Eastern library, found remnants telling of the antediluvian world and fish creatures which spent their days with the humans but belonged to the ocean and went there at night, and one day did not return.

He climbs the stairs and gets into bed, lying on sandy sheets with second-hand books beneath the mattress. He closes his eyes and colours swell, bleeding tentacles, becoming sea anemones. He breathes deeply. Eventually, he falls asleep. When he wakes in the night, the sea is pounding the cliffs, like someone thumping at the door, wanting him.

He wakes again at dawn, gets up and goes downstairs. He can see, through the kitchen doorway, his unused supper things still out on the table. He can hear, on the radio, the shipping forecast, the strange language of the sea – *moving slowly, moving deep, losing its identity.*

He opens the door to the shower room in which his father's black neoprene wetsuit still hangs. He touches it, smells it.

In the understairs cupboard, he finds the cool lead and the cylinder with its dregs of old air.

He struggles down to the beach and over the sand, the tank

heavy on his back. The tide is out but turning. He makes his way to the edge of the vast and shifting sea, where life perhaps began. Between the hazy sky and the hazy sea, he can see no horizon. Salt water laps over his feet. He steps forward, leaving webbed footprints in the damp sand. He wades deeper. The sea worms in beneath his wetsuit, getting in at the neck. (An early-morning dog-walker glimpses his head resting on the surface of the water like a buoy. A wave rises between them.) He sinks down. (When the wave falls, there is nothing there but the stone-grey sea, and daylight touching its surface. She walks on, beneath the crumbling cliff path and an old house facing the creeping tide.)

Monsoon Puddles

'CAN ANYONE FIND a corner to fill?'
My mother's phrase, my mother's voice, my mother's hands stacking the plates. My mother's phrase on her sister's lips; twin voices, twin hands. My mother is gone, but Aunty Frances fills a corner. She says I can help her home with her dishes; she'll run me back afterwards.

Dad says, 'Wait until the end. You can't leave halfway through.'

Aunty Frances mutters something under her nicotine breath. I don't catch it, but I can almost see it – an acrid fog hanging on her lips. Dad turns away. He doesn't smoke, and hates the stench which will cling to him, particles lingering on his skin and in his hair like tenacious burrs. He will change, he will wash; but still he will catch a waft, or he will think that others can.

She smuggles me out. She says a wake is no place for a child. In the passenger seat of her car, I stiffly embrace the precarious load teetering on my narrow lap, travelling anxiously with breakables rattling beneath my fingertips. When we reach her house, she takes these empties and leftovers from me and carries them less carefully inside. Her hallway smells like smouldering flowers. She puts the dishes down on the kitchen table. 'Did you try these?' she asks, pointing to a tray of sampled and abandoned savouries. I shake my head. She feeds me some. 'Pakora. It's Indian.'

She asks if my father ever talks about his trip to India.

I didn't know he had been.

'We went together,' she explains. 'We worked on the same magazine. I was a features writer.' My father is a photographer. She takes my hand and tours me around her living room, showing off her colourful tapestries and carved wooden boxes and statues.

I ask her about the elephant man on her mantelpiece.

'That's Ganesha,' she says, 'remover of obstacles and patron of learning. His father, Shiva, was commanded to cut the head off the first thing he saw, which unfortunately was his own son. But then he saved Ganesha's life by replacing his lost head with an elephant's.'

I am appalled by this image of a father who listens to the voices compelling him to do such heinous things, and the bodged repair which maybe he hopes nobody will notice. *Head? What head?*

'Would you like to try some Indian tea?' she asks. She boils up milk with herbs and spices, and we drink the *chai* from small, hot glasses.

The train journey from Bombay to Surat takes about six hours. I sit on a hard bench, writing notes. Beside me is an Indian man who reads over my shoulder and stops me every now and again to correct my spelling of the names of the places we pass through. Beside him sits his mother who peels small oranges and includes me when she shares out the segments. Later, the son moves to the opposite bench to let his mother lie down, and she lies with her head on her shawl at the far end and her bare feet resting on my thigh.

John sits on another bench trying to explain to some men what he does for a living, with his very little Hindi and their very little English. He gestures taking photographs, and then gets out a copy of the magazine and shows them pictures of male models with his name beneath them. They pretend to misunderstand him, shaking their heads in refusal to believe that he is the man in the photograph.

The train rattles on for hours through the smells and sounds of many different stations, many different villages. When we stop, traders board with baskets of fruit and bread and pots of hot chai; and beggars with limbs as thin and knotty as their sticks; and a leper, who is beaten away by the policemen.

When my legs and backside become stiff and begin to ache, I stand up, placing the woman's bare feet gently down on the bench. She tuts loudly. I inch through the standing passengers, all men, to the open doorway, and stand there cooling in the rush of fresh air. At each station, the breeze wilts and a rank smell leaks through the toilet door into the carriage, burning my nostrils.

I return to the bench where the woman is peeling more oranges. She holds a piece out to me, the juice dripping down her long, thin fingers and onto my white trousers.

When my father phones, I say to him, 'Kemcho. Tamaru naam su che?'

'I'm coming to pick you up,' he says, and puts the phone down.

Again, in the car, I try this Gujarati greeting, these phrases my Aunty Frances has taught me: *Hello. What is your name? Maru naam Jenny che.* He doesn't respond. From the back seat, I watch his eyes in the rear-view mirror, flicking back and forth and from side to side, from the road ahead to the road behind, to me, and away again. His eyes are brown with a sliver of amber; his lids are heavy; he looks sad even when he smiles. I don't have his eyes; mine are blue like my mother's and Aunty Frances's. I ask, 'Did mum ever go?'

'Where?'

'To India.'

'No.' He switches on the radio. The subject is closed.

I dream that night of Ganesha, who stands before me with his elephant's head bearing down on his skinny body, its weight too great for his legs, which look like they might buckle. He plants his bare feet wide to keep his balance and fixes me with his elephant eyes, which are brown, with a chink of amber; the lids are heavy and make him look sad. And Shiva is begging Ganesha not to tell anybody what he has done.

We are in India for a couple of weeks to produce an article on a wedding in a village in Gujarat, a bus-ride north of Surat.

The bride's name is Pritti. We capture her first in her daily routine before the wedding preparations start. Down by the river at dawn, John takes the photographs and I conduct an interview, while Pritti washes clothes, beating shirts so hard against the rocks that the buttons break off. She makes chappatis, rolling them and putting them out to dry on mats in the early sun, where they become pock-marked with the footprints of tiny birds which run through the dust and over the chappatis. Her brothers and sisters want to practise their English on us, but they only know how to ask our names, so conversations sound like Rumpelstiltskin riddles. In the evenings, we return to our guest house, where we eat and sleep to the sound of the cicadas, the helicopter beetles and the call to prayer.

The guest house is a family business managed by a middle-aged couple and their unmarried daughter, Sangita. Monkeys sit on the roof, watching our comings and goings. John and I have a bedroom each, and every morning Sangita brings us chai.

She tells John that it is not proper for him to visit the bride at home on the eve of her wedding. We agree that I will go alone to document the wedding party preparations, while John goes off to take contextual pictures, landscapes, whatever takes his eye. I eat with the bride and her family, and return to the guest house late. John is not in his room. I fall asleep, and by the time I wake the next morning, John is already out and about.

I return to Pritti's house. Everybody is busy dressing and decorating the bride. One of her sisters paints my hands with cold dots of henna paste, making concentric circles on each palm, and a flower in the middle, painting bangles around my wrists and rings around my fingers.

I am expecting to see John at the wedding, but he is not there. I take some pictures on my own camera and wait for him to arrive, but he doesn't come. He misses the wedding and the day of celebration which follows it. I collect a roll of thirty-six snaps with people's heads and feet chopped off or with my thumb half over the lens. I forget the flash in a dim room or face the sun, which scorches out the image. My record of the occasion is skewed and blurry.

When I finally catch up with John, he makes a few lame excuses. He says we can tell the magazine that I or he took the pictures while he was ill.

As it happens, John is not ill at all, not once. It is me who goes down with terrible diarrhoea and vomiting the day after the celebrations. I stay at home feeling wretched, sleeping and sweating and washing, watching my orange henna patterns fade.

John goes out every morning to get bottles of water and Thums Up! cola for me before going to work. Each evening I ask him for the day's stories; whether there are interviews I need to do to accompany his pictures; whether he has written down all the subjects' names. In response, he is vague; he says he has photographed nothing worthwhile that day but will go out again the next day.

On the third day of my illness I am feeling a little better and a little bored. In the afternoon, I get up and go to John's room. He is still out, but while I wait for him to return, I sit down to look at the Polaroids spread out on his bed. I am expecting to see pictures of the village and its surroundings, the market and the shrines, the main road and its traffic. I am surprised and puzzled to find myself looking at dozens of pictures of Sangita down by the river, stained orange by the sunrise.

When I talk about going to India, Dad says, 'Bloody Frances.' He says I am too young, and that I don't have the money. This is true when I am fourteen with a paper-round, but not when I am eighteen and working, with Aunty Frances topping up my fund for my nineteenth birthday. 'Bloody Frances,' he says. He thought I had forgotten all about it, that I had left India behind. Still he tries to put me off, to find reasons for me not to go. 'You'll get ill,' he says. 'Frances was very ill when she was there.'

'Yes,' I say, 'she told me. But you weren't.'

He looks startled.

⚘

There are more than a hundred photographs of Sangita altogether. Beneath the stack of pictures of her looking fresh and shy in the morning sunshine there is another collection. In these, her sari is a little dishevelled, her hair is a little tousled, her face is a little flushed, and her smile is a little secret.

I confront John when he comes home. He is embarrassed and defensive.

'How could you?' I ask. 'What about Linda? Does Sangita know you're married?'

'Yes, she knows,' he says.

'And what are you planning on doing? What are you going to tell Linda?'

'Linda doesn't need to know,' he says.

I turn away.

On the day we leave, while we are waiting to catch the bus back to Surat, I see Sangita running through the village in an orange sari, scattering the dust and the chickens. She catches up with us and holds John's hands and face and tells him he must stay.

I stand at a distance, turned away, angry with both of them. John makes excuses and promises, all the while squinting into the distance, looking for the bus, which eventually comes. As it pulls away we stare back at Sangita who stands horribly alone, shrinking in the dust, becoming a puddle of orange in the distance as we travel away along the bumpy road.

Neither of us tells Linda, although she notices that he does not like to talk about India, and perhaps she notices how I have cooled towards my brother-in-law. She suggests to me that his illness was a particularly bad experience for him.

'Poor John,' I say.

She says she hopes that he wasn't too difficult a patient.
'Not at all,' I say.

In the monsoon season, the river swells and stays fat for months, lurking at the edge of the village, watched and monitored and speculated about, and then it shrinks again, leaving behind puddles and the debris of the flood.

I pack long skirts, loose trousers, long-sleeved tops, a hat, sunscreen, mosquito repellent, malaria tablets. I have my ticket, visa, money, and an address.

I travel in December, when England's winter is wet and grey, and India's is orange. I make the journey Frances has described to me, flying at dawn into Bombay. The roads are already swollen with traffic – black and yellow taxis and auto-rickshaws weaving between lorries and bicycles and camels with carts. The air is thick with the honking of horns and the ringing of bells, and nonchalant cows potter across four rough lanes of traffic, playing lazy chicken.

I catch a train to Surat, breaking up my journey with tea and fruit, and in Surat I catch a bus, a boneshaker which deposits me on a dusty roadside at the end of the afternoon.

Approaching the village is like approaching Neverland or Oz, a place which only exists in stories. There is the river which will flood in the summer. And there is the guest house with grey monkeys loitering on the roof as if they were no more exotic than pigeons.

The girl at the desk is on the phone. I wait. She is about my age, I think. Behind her, a door opens into a back room, where a middle-aged woman sits in front of a glassless window, with the shutters wide open and the early evening sunlight dancing around her. Her eyes are closed. The girl behind the desk puts down the phone. She lifts her head, raising her heavy eyelids and looking at me with eyes which are dark brown with a sliver of amber.

'What is your name?' she asks, searching for my answer in her ledger.

In the back room, the melting sun drips warm orange puddles into the dozing woman's lap, and the folds of her sari ripple as she stirs.

It Has Happened Before

ELEANOR, THINKS ROGER, is in love with the postman. Roger lunches regularly at Eleanor's house and sees how she watches her driveway through the kitchen window, distracted from their conversation, alert to the approach of this striking young man who comes with the mail in the early afternoon, ensuring that when he does come, she is near the front door.

Or, there is somebody else in her life, from whom she anticipates love letters, gifts; someone she's hiding from Roger. Except that nothing ever comes for her. She receives nothing but junk.

The postman is at least ten years younger than her. If Eleanor is in love with the postman, she is making a fool of herself, thinks Roger, who is older than her.

It has happened before. Roger's own mother had a fling with the milkman. And Rosemary down the road was recently discovered, by her husband Victor, fucking the gardener on the kitchen floor. Victor walked out after that, late one night or early one morning – Rosemary woke up and found him gone. Victor took almost nothing, but he did take his wallet, so he is probably holed up in a hotel somewhere, punishing her.

Roger used to work a late shift in a factory out of town, getting home in the early hours and sleeping until noon. He is retired now but still sleeps late.

Rising much later today than he meant to, and full of bad

dreams, somewhat shaken, he opens his curtains and peers across the road to see if Eleanor is in her kitchen having lunch. If she hasn't already eaten, she might like to join him.

Eleanor, though, is not in her kitchen. She is standing on the pavement outside her house, crying in front of the postman, holding on to his sleeve, begging him; and he, the postman, touching Eleanor's arm, nods.

Roger turns away from the window and goes downstairs. He puts his coat on over his pyjamas and swaps his slippers for shoes. Leaving the house, he finds Eleanor already gone, the postman too. At the end of his driveway, Roger stops, looking up and down the street, but no one is there.

He crosses the road to Eleanor's house and knocks on her door but she doesn't answer. He looks through her windows but doesn't see her. Returning to his house, he telephones, letting it ring, but she doesn't pick up. He watches her house for a while, an hour. He doesn't think she's there. He thinks about her crying and the postman touching her.

It occurs to Roger that he knows where the postman lives. He has driven past the postman's house many times, heading out to the factory.

He misses working. He has plans, involving Eleanor or Europe, but he has so far just been sleeping his mornings away. He plays the lottery every week, hoping for a jackpot. It happens – why shouldn't it happen to him?

He had planned, before sleeping so late, to make lunch for Eleanor today, for her birthday. He has bought flowers; they are waiting in water.

The postman's house stands alone at the edge of town. It is just about the last thing you see as you leave. He has seen the postman sitting on his front doorstep wearing a string vest and shorts, or just shorts, drinking beer.

Roger puts on proper trousers, and a jumper under his coat – it is midwinter; it is frosty out there. Getting into his car, he drives to the outskirts.

What does he expect to find? Eleanor, in the postman's bed? He found the milkman in his mother's.

He would like to find letters and parcels, undelivered mail piled high, kids' birthday cards ripped open for the cash. Then the postman would be sacked; he would be sent away.

Or knickers. A collection of knickers from the local women's washing lines. Someone has been stealing ladies underwear as it hangs drying.

He has no idea what he might find.

Roger drives slowly past the postman's house and parks down a track before walking back. There is no car in the postman's driveway. There is a garage whose door is shut. Roger doesn't know whether the postman has a car or just a bike. He crouches in the bushes at the side of the house. At least he doesn't need to worry about being seen by neighbours. He waits, watching. He has a view of both the front door and the side door but no one goes in and no one leaves. He notes that the curtains in the upstairs windows are closed.

He takes out his cigarettes. He has tried to give up – Eleanor doesn't like him smoking – but withdrawal gives him the shakes.

When he gets too cold and stiff, when the light starts to go, when he can no longer bear the smell of the shrubs, the jabbing of sharp branches, when he runs out of cigarettes, he stands. He is, he has decided, going in.

He is lucky, he thinks: the side door is not locked. Roger lets himself in, closing the door quietly behind him. He walks through the dim kitchen, through the buzzing of electricity, into the hallway. He looks at the shoe rack and the coat pegs, seeing nothing of Eleanor's, only men's things.

He steps onto the stairs, the bottom step, which creaks, and Roger wonders whether there is anyone in the upstairs rooms to hear. He wants to turn back now. He doesn't want to know, he tells himself, but he keeps on moving, climbing up the gloomy stairs to the landing. He has no idea what he is going to find.

There are three doors. A bathroom, he supposes, and a bedroom or two, perhaps a bedroom and a spare room, the room in which the postman keeps the hoarded mail and the stolen knickers.

He reaches for the nearest doorknob and pauses, steeling himself.

When he turns it, opening the door, he finds a bedroom in darkness. He can discern, though, someone naked, face-down on the bed. Crossing to the window, he draws aside the curtain, but all daylight has gone now. He feels for the light switch, turning on spotlights trained on the bed, finding Victor, Rosemary's Victor, on a waterproof sheet.

Roger gets close to Victor's face, which is turned towards him, his cheek against the heavy-duty plastic. When Victor tries to speak, Roger sees how dry his lips are. He has the mouth of a man who is dying in the desert. And then Victor's eyes swivel towards the door, and Roger looks too and sees the postman in the doorway, his uniform off, a beer bottle in his hand.

❦

When Eleanor leaves her sister's house, it is dark, which is a relief. She must, she thinks, look frightful. But she has splashed her face with cold water and combed her hair. She has calmed down.

She walks home, goes into her kitchen and puts on the light.

She can at least talk about it with her sister, who understands, of course, because it is her big brother, too, who has gone missing.

It has happened before. He went missing during his first term at university, leaving without a word and returning with a tan the following summer. He ran away on his wedding day and didn't come home for six months. But he always sends a postcard, a birthday card, a Christmas card. Not this time though; it's been a year now.

His absence has stirred in their mother a memory of the men who, in her youth, went to France and Belgium and never came back. Their small town, over time, was stripped of men. A whole generation, just gone.

Eleanor looks at the mail, the junk, on her kitchen counter, and throws it away.

She is all right now, she thinks. She will go to bed.

It will strike her, when she is all tucked up, that she has not seen Roger, but she will not get out of bed to call him, to see how he is, to suggest lunch the following day. She will already have taken a sleeping pill, and anyway – she will glance at her digital alarm clock glowing red in the dark – it will be too late.

The Yacht Man

WHEN THE MAN arrives, Linda invites him inside. She shows him into the living room and offers him a seat on the sofa as she sits down, but he prefers to stand.

She says, 'I need a door.'

She has looked in B&Q but wants something a bit different. His Yellow Pages advert stood out. She thought he would bring a catalogue from which she could choose the type of wood she wants, the type of handle. She has considered stained-glass panels. But he doesn't have a catalogue for her to browse through. What he has in his hands, what he opens and places on the table between them, is a display book full of pictures of the astonishingly fine work he once did on a yacht. He shows her pages of gracefully curving and gleaming mahogany chests of drawers and cabinets. She admires his work and he is pleased.

She offers him a cup of tea but he wants water. Colin, keeping out of the way in the kitchen, fills a glass and the kettle.

The yacht man, turning the page, shows Linda various views of exquisite marquetry. She touches the pictures with her fingertips, as if she might be able to feel that smooth, exotic wood.

The sturdy, beech-effect table on which the book lies is not beautiful but it was the practical choice while the kids were young. They have grown up and gone now though. She recently brought down from the loft a lovely side table which she has put in the hallway.

She found it at a flea market. This was before Colin, when she was with Vincent. Her eye was drawn to some engagement and eternity rings, and a table with Queen Anne legs, and she said to Vincent, 'What do you think?' But when she looked around, he was elsewhere, looking at a diving helmet. She bought the table anyway. A few years later, she heard that Vincent was living on a marine research vessel in the middle of some ocean.

'It's all very nice,' says Linda, 'but I just need a door.'

'I can do a door,' he says, without looking up from his photographs. He seems disappointed.

He takes measurements in the hallway, but when he leaves he still hasn't shown her a single front door.

After locking up behind him, Linda returns to the living room. She and Colin have supper in front of the television and go up to bed.

In the morning, she finds the yacht man's water glass on the table in the hallway, and the mark it has left on the wood.

She won't call him. She will look again in the Yellow Pages for someone who can make her an ordinary door, something solid, attractive enough, inexpensive. Perhaps she will go back to B&Q. In the meantime, and afterwards, she will – with partial success – try to remove that perfect white circle on the Queen Anne table where the yacht man placed his glass before he left.

The Machines

THERE IS A factory behind Christine's house going twenty-four hours a day. In the middle of the night, when she is awake in the otherwise silent house, she can hear the rhythmic clanking of the machines. At other times, she might think that she can't hear them, but this is only because she is getting used to it. At the back of everything, the noise is still there; it is constant.

She worked in the factory when she was eighteen, in between school and university. There were three shifts a day, and it was not uncommon to work a double. All summer, she heard the machines in her sleep. She still dreams about the factory sometimes.

The machines were alarming – these rows of huge steel contraptions with parts banging up and down and other bits zipping left and right, this going underneath that, and that slamming down. Some sections of the production line were less clankingly noisy but perhaps all the more disquieting, components shooting smoothly down and then up again, leaving behind perfect holes. It was one of these machines which once took a woman's fingers off. So you had to be careful.

Her dad used to work there as well, and when he retired he found the world too quiet and still. Her parents lived where they had always lived, some miles out of town, just where the farms started. Sometimes you could only hear birds, maybe something in the distance, the buzz of a lawnmower, the bleating of sheep. The sheep made a racket during lambing, and again when the lambs were taken away a few months later. Their bleating then was like the sounding of klaxons. Afterwards, there was hush.

Even the machines in the house, said her father to her mother without having to raise his voice above the sound of the vacuum cleaner, made very little noise. He helped with the housework, loading the dishwasher and the washing machine and setting both running at the same time, but still there was only a gentle background hum which did not even necessitate turning up Classic FM. When it was too quiet, he talked to himself, or to his mother, who was no longer alive. He rediscovered heavy metal, getting out all his old tapes, and he got into *Robot Wars*, which filled the silence.

He died while Christine was at university, knocked down by rush-hour traffic in the nearest town. She got the train home on a Sunday and her mother picked her up from the station. The town centre, as they drove through it, was deserted. Christine put the radio on.

She laid claim to her dad's tapes. She found a Walkman and listened to her dad's heavy metal in bed and on the train on the return journey.

After university, she moved back home and got a job in a call centre. She started dating someone who worked in the cubicle next to hers. They ate their lunch together and talked about going to China before everything changed, or getting a couple of round-the-world tickets and just taking off, escaping. Instead, they got married and got a mortgage on a small house on the outskirts of town.

The only grass near this house is at the cemetery. They have a concrete backyard, and empty pots in which Christine might grow tomatoes. The front door opens right onto the street. The traffic is nonstop during the day, dirtying the brickwork and the white plastic door and the front windows, which Christine has to keep closed so that the net curtains don't get filthy. It is a far cry from the peace of her childhood home.

Christine had always been a good sleeper, but after she got pregnant she began to wake in the middle of the night for no apparent reason, or with cramps in her legs, or with hunger pangs, cravings, at three or four or five o'clock in the morning. She would have to get up and go down to the kitchen, through whose window she could see the factory which never slept. People had all sorts of advice for remedying the insomnia and the cramps – warm baths, milk with honey, yoga – but at the same time, people were inclined to say, 'Get used to it. You'll never again sleep the way you used to.'

Even so, when the baby was born, the sleep deprivation came as a shock. He wanted her breast almost constantly and woke every two hours during the night until four or five in the morning when he was ready to get up. This was in the winter, when it was still dark, with hours of darkness to come. She tried taking him into her bed but he did not like it. She tried walking around with him, singing to him, rocking him, all of which he liked but he did not go back to sleep. So then she put a light on, made a cup of tea and half-listened to the World Service programmes which come on before the shipping forecast. But even after a cup of tea, and even with the radio on, her eyes kept closing. Reading to him, she would blink and slip into sleep, having micro-dreams between one sentence and the next.

In the spring, she found that she was waking to that beautiful blue the still-starry sky turns just before dawn. By the end of May and well into July, the sun had already risen when the baby got her up.

After feeding him, she began to take him out in the pram, wheeling him along the canal towpath until the sound of the factory's midnight to eight am shift was almost too far away to hear. On the road, the first buses went past, empty. She did not go anywhere in particular – the park did not open until seven and none of the cafés opened before eight – but she enjoyed the walk and the fresh air.

When the summer came to an end, she was once again waking up in the dark. But she began to appreciate the fact that she had not missed the sunrise, and that she could feed the baby and then dawn would arrive and she still had time to walk somewhere and see the sun come up.

She had a few favourite places. Sometimes she went no further than the canal, stopping on the bridge – putting the brakes on the pram – and sitting on the wall to watch the dingy water's transformation at sunrise. Sometimes she wheeled him up to the monument and sat on its steps. But this morning, she headed for the new supermarket. Overlooked on one side by old office blocks, the area itself was unattractive, but on a clear day there was a good view to the east.

The twenty-four-hour supermarket looked abandoned when she went in. There was no one on the tills. When she got further into the store, she saw a few people stacking the shelves. She found herself tailed by a security guard, who kept an eye on her the whole time she was in there. She picked up a pack of nappies and then went to the fridge and got herself a drink, an iced coffee to keep herself awake. The security guard watched her even while she was paying for her things at the self-service checkout. When she put the nappies under the pram she felt guilty, as if she were doing something wrong, stashing these goods and wheeling them out of his shop.

Back outside, she parked the pram beside a bench and sat down with her coffee. She could not hear the factories now. She wanted to listen to one of her dad's old heavy metal compilations – she had the Walkman in her bag with a tape already inside it. Digging out the headphones and putting them on, she pressed 'play' and waited for the sun to rise.

She opens her eyes. There is no sound coming from her headphones. Lifting her chin from her chest, she looks at the Walkman and sees that the tape has played out. It was probably the music ending, the silence and then the Walkman switching itself off, which disturbed her.

She turns to look at the baby, looking at the place where the baby should be. There is nothing there but slabs. She turns to look at the other side of the bench even though she knows she did not put the pram there. She stands. Her bag drops quietly to the floor and the plug is pulled from the Walkman so that the headphones remain on her head but with nothing at the end of the dangling lead.

When the woman in the factory lost her fingers, somebody stopped the machines. The production line came to a halt but there was all this yelling which filled the silence, and there was a frenzy of activity, people all trying to do something which would help. Christine remembers someone bringing lumps of ice for the woman's hand, for the woman's fingers.

But more than the accident and all the hysteria which followed it, what she mostly remembers is how it was afterwards, when the woman had been taken away and all the shouting and screaming had stopped and everyone was beginning to go back to whatever they had been doing before.

Wink Wink

MY FATHER MEETS me off the train, takes my bag and guides me to the car.

'How long have we got you for?' he asks.

'A couple of weeks,' I say. 'Then I have to get back.'

'How's everything?' he asks. 'How's the new house?'

'Oh fine,' I say, 'except for the window. We've boarded it up for now.'

'The window?' he says. 'What happened?'

'Oh,' I say, 'we just had a bit of trouble. Some lads on their way back from the pub broke a window. I told Mum on the phone last night – did she not tell you?'

Of course my mother has not told him. She even said, 'I don't think I'll tell your father. It would upset him, to think of you having trouble like that.'

It is like they are playing a game, seeing how many secrets they can stack up against one another. They both do it: *Don't tell your father, it will only worry him. Your mother doesn't need to know; it's our little secret.*

One Saturday afternoon when my mother was at work and my father was looking after me, he drove me to the cinema and bought me a ticket to see *Grease*, a film my mother did not want me to see. He gave me money for sweets, counting the coins into my hand, just as he used to give me a little bit extra when the fair was on, putting it into my pocket as I headed out of the back door. 'Don't tell your mother,' he said, and went *wink wink*. After the film, he collected me from the foyer and we went home. He looked a bit guilty – worried, I assumed, that I would tell my mother about his treat, but I didn't.

We pull into the driveway of my parents' house. My mother is already in the doorway, waiting for us. I get out of the car and give her a hug and am surprised by her grey hairs and the smallness of her body in my arms.

'Look,' she says, ushering me into the house and pushing a carrier bag at me. 'I got you something in the sales.'

I peer into the bag and see pink bulging up at me. I pull it out, a shocking pink dress which my mother takes and holds up against me and says, 'There.'

She goes to hang it up in my room.

'Will you wear it?' asks my father, quietly in the hallway. 'Just while you're here?'

I pull a face.

'I know,' he says, laughing, 'but do it for your mother.'

I accept my assignment.

He says, 'Good chap,' and goes *wink wink*.

I take my bag and go up to my room.

'Maybe it's a bit bright,' says my mother, 'but your father likes to see you in a dress.'

I remember her, brown-haired and not so little, stopping me on the landing and giving me a fiver for a few more rides at the fair. 'Don't tell your father,' she said, *wink wink*, and I carried our little secret down to the kitchen and found my father waiting there with pound coins. *Wink wink*.

When I was little, my father let me creep downstairs after

my mother had gone to sleep. I sat on his knee watching late-night telly and he whispered, 'For God's sake, don't tell your mother.' And on his club nights, when my father was out having a few drinks with his old workmates, my mother gave me sips of her gin and orange before bed, and said, 'You don't need to tell your father.' *Wink wink.*

When I've been home for a few days, I am sitting up late in the lounge reading a magazine and eating toast. I hear my father returning home from the social club. His key slips into the lock without any fumbling, and he lets himself in with none of the usual noise and buffoonery made when drunk and trying to be quiet. He closes the front door gently behind him and I hear him taking off his coat and shoes. Then, following the lamplight and the sound of page-turning and toast-munching, he comes into the lounge, looking surprised and saying, 'Oh!' when he sees me sitting there.

'Hi Dad,' I say.

'I've just been at the club,' he says, glancing down at himself.

'I know,' I say. 'Are you stopping up? Do you want to watch something?'

'No,' he says, shaking his head and putting his hands in his pockets. He looks like a reluctant little boy. 'No, I'm going to bed.'

But still he stands there until I say, 'Night then.'

'Night, love,' he says, and he comes over to give me a good-night kiss. He leans over and I wait for the smell of drink and cigarette smoke to hit me – the club has always made him reek of both – but he smells very nice. When he kisses me, he kisses a small furrow of query in my forehead. He says again, 'Night, love,' and as he turns to leave the room he smiles down at me and winks.

Over breakfast, we listen to the news on the radio. There is an item about a young man who made a lot of money for his company through illegal means, and at his trial it emerged that his company had been well aware of his activities but pretended not to know as he was making them so much money.

'How ridiculous,' says my mother. 'Fancy letting someone get up to no good right under your nose and not saying a word.'

I whack my spoon down on the shell of my boiled egg and set about peeling it off.

'I'm going through to watch *Country File*,' my mother says, taking her cup of tea with her.

I eat my egg, watching my father, who rubs his nose and reads his paper. Then I get up and follow my mother through to the lounge where I find her in front of the drinks cabinet adding a nip of gin to her tea.

'Just a dash,' she says gaily when she sees me out of the corner of her eye. She tests her tea and closes the cabinet. 'Don't tell your father.' *Wink wink*. She switches the telly on and stares sadly at John Craven. 'He's a lovely man,' she says.

'. . . pioneering a social change . . .' says John.

'A good man.'

'. . . that will transform the landscape . . .'

'But he needs his Saturdays out.'

'Well,' I say, 'he's always gone to the club.'

My mother sips at her tea.

'Coming up next . . .' says John.

I am in town on market day, squinting through the autumn sun as I browse, rubbing fabrics between my fingers, picking up cheap paperbacks, the end-of-day shouts repeating like poetry in my ears:

Five pound bag for a pound bananas
Two pound a pound on your seedless grapes
Four cauliflower for a pound now ladies
Two pound o' mushroom for a quid.

I am eye to dead eye with a rabbit strung up on the butcher's stall when I catch sight of my father. I make my way through the market crowd, my father dipping in and out of view until he is close enough to hear me say, 'Hi Dad.' Panic flits across his face.

He says, 'Cathy!' as if he has not seen me in years. He is with another man but does not introduce me.

'I thought you were going to the club.'

'I'm just on my way there now,' he says, like a boy found dawdling to school.

'I'll see you later then.' I head home and my father goes in the other direction, taking a long way round to the club.

My mother is lying on the sofa. The television is on but she is asleep. Half a cup of tea is on the table in front of her and the bottle of gin is empty. I switch the television off and my mother wakes up with a start.

'John?' she says.

'It's me, Mum,' I say.

'Oh, hello, love. I was just having a little lie down. What time is it?'

'It's about six. I've just got back from town. I saw Dad.'

'Did you? Who was he with?'

'No one I know. A man with a ginger beard.'

My mother nods.

'He said he was just off to the club.'

'It's not there any more, you know,' she says as I sit down next to her. 'The club's gone. They knocked it down. It's a car park now. He still goes,' she adds, and starts to laugh and laughs until she says, 'Oh dear.' I notice then that the sofa cushions are warm and wet beneath us, and there is a weak smell of urine in the air. 'Don't tell your father,' she says, looking at me and slowly closing and opening one eye, red-rimmed from the gin-soaked nap and maybe crying.

Wink wink.

If There's Anything Left

AQUEUE HAS formed on the narrow staircase, a build-up of other hotel guests trying to get down to the breakfast room. James, waiting at the bottom, observing Kath's steady progress, is reminded of a tractor or a learner driver tailed by an impatient push of rush-hour traffic.

Someone says to someone else, 'There'll be nothing left by the time we get there.' They do not say this quietly.

Kath used to be so thin, too thin, James thought. He joked about losing her in the bed. His friends called her a catch and his father called her a keeper but even after they were married James often felt as if he were still trying to catch her. She was always so busy, forever dashing off somewhere or going on ahead.

Since the accident, though, she has slowed right down and she has put on weight. Now she always seems to be eating and her clothes are a size larger than his mother's. James knows that even as they make their way down to breakfast, she will have in her jacket pocket an emergency bag of sweets to suck on.

When Kath finally reaches the bottom of the stairs, people overtake her on both sides like a school of fish parting around an obstacle or a potential predator, before coming together again. Kath stops and waits until they have all gone, and then she moves forward towards the dining room.

It is not an expensive hotel – it is small, smaller than

he remembers, and a bit run-down – but it is right on the seafront. They came here last summer. It seems longer ago. After breakfast, they might sit outside on the bench, an uncomfortable ironwork two-seater. Kath wants to walk along the beach to the pier, from the end of which they watched last summer's sunsets. She wants to take Zac there.

Yesterday, they had their lunchtime fish and chips on the bench, watching the seagulls going after the scraps. Afterwards, on the beach, Kath stripped off to her modest underwear, having come to the seaside without a bikini, and James turned away from her empty breasts. He supposes that the scar from her Caesarean is almost invisible now. Her other scars have healed well.

Kath wandered down to the edge of the sea, putting her feet in the water, while James sat on his towel fully clothed. Before he lay back, he saw her reach around and unhook her bra, slipping it off her shoulders and dropping it onto the stones behind her. He saw her removing her knickers and throwing them down too. He watched her walking out. When she was up to her waist – and still going deeper, even though, he thought, it had to be cold – he lay down and closed his eyes.

When he woke up, he had no idea how much time had passed. He felt as if he had been asleep for ages, but the sun was still high in the cloud-covered sky – he could see the blurry brightness of it trying to burn through. It had been a cool week. He wanted a heatwave, that melting feeling.

He sat up. He could see a distant figure in the sea. It was probably Kath. He could not tell whether she was still swimming out or heading in. He stood up and got back onto the prom, leaving his beach towel behind. He had not weighted it in any way. It occurred to him that he would have liked to look back and see it blowing away down the beach. He did not turn around.

He went back to the hotel room and then to the pub. This morning, he remembered standing at the bar with some man who said to him, 'What's in the bag?'

In the dining room, Kath goes straight to the hot buffet while James sees what fruit juice is left. Each morning, the proprietor puts out jugs filled to the brim, but he does not replenish them. When it is gone it is gone. The orange juice always goes first. James takes the last of the grapefruit juice to their table. Kath, sitting down with a full English breakfast, says to him, 'Are you going to eat?' James looks at the food on her plate but it turns his stomach; there is nothing there that he could face.

Kath never used to be very interested in food, or didn't have time for it. These days she bakes; she makes big meals and James has to tell her that he is not hungry. He goes off to work without any breakfast and does not come home from the pub in time for dinner. She asks him what he has eaten and sometimes he makes something up, something nourishing and warming, because it's what she wants to hear. He doesn't always do this though; he doesn't always tell her what she wants to hear.

It was Kath's idea to come here. 'Getting away' she called it, but that depends on what you're trying to get away from. What he wants is to be back at work. Kath is keen for him to look for a new job, something which would not entail such increasingly long hours, such a tiring drive. Then, she says, he wouldn't have to leave the house almost as soon as they get up. 'We'd have more time together in the mornings,' she tells him. 'We could meet up for lunch.'

James, though, does not want something closer to home. He does not want a job which starts later and finishes earlier and enables him to see Kath at lunchtime. He likes his job, he says.

They chose their house because of its convenience for Kath's work. He remembers her telling people that all she had to do was zip down the A road, that she could be at work in ten minutes flat.

'There's a thirty zone in the middle, though,' said James, 'which slows you down.'

Someone said, 'It won't slow Kath down,' and people laughed.

He remembers going to view their house when the estate was being built, when Kath was newly pregnant and waking up in the mornings feeling nauseous, with an ache in her breasts. The house was empty, all bare boards and bare walls and echo and the garden was a long stretch of bare, frozen mud. There was a show house which they went to see, so that they could imagine how theirs might look, with a dining table set for a family meal, and bunk beds in the second bedroom.

Even the baby didn't slow her down. Soon bored of being at home, Kath got back to work as quickly as she could, whizzing first to the nursery with Zac and dropping him off before dashing to work, desperate for office life.

James wonders whether the barrier has been repaired yet. These things can take a long time. Kath told him that someone had left a bouquet of flowers next to the damaged post. 'They still had the cellophane on,' she said. 'I think they'd look nicer without the cellophane, don't you? When the flowers die it will just be litter.'

Kath clears her plate and struggles to her feet, going back to the buffet for more. The hot breakfast dishes are almost empty. She scrapes what she can from them. James looks over at the fruit juice table but there is only one jug left and it contains what looks like tomato juice, which he does not want; it would not be quenching.

When Kath is sitting down again, James says to her, 'I walked along the beach last night.' She picks up her cutlery. He says, 'I went to the pier.'

From the look on her face, he knows she has realised what he is telling her, that it is sinking in. She is getting to her feet again. She is going to go all the way up those stairs to their bedroom to look on the dressing table, to see what is or isn't there.

'The urn's empty,' he says, but she is going anyway. She has to see for herself.

He remembers the man in the pub saying, 'Most of the body becomes gas. It just goes. You don't bring it home with you.'

James leaves the dining room too, but he turns away from the stairs and heads outside, his eyes watering as he emerges from the relative dinge into weak sunlight. Sitting down on the filigree loveseat, he puts his hand to his breast pocket, wanting his sunglasses, but they're not there.

Static

WILFRED TAKES THE dirty teacup from the bedside table. Dorothy's eyes are closed, but she is still awake, just resting. The gilt-edged, rose-print Duchess has seen better days. The inside is stained with tannin and the gilding is worn.

'I'll be back with a fresh one,' he says. He closes the bedroom door behind him and climbs slowly down the stairs, the bone china cup trembling on its saucer.

In the kitchen, he puts the used teacup in the empty stainless steel sink and stands for a few minutes looking out of the window into the back garden. They have lived in this house their whole married life. From time to time, Dorothy has suggested moving – sometimes to another town or to the countryside, sometimes to the sea or even abroad. They could even travel, she said, now that their children were grown up and no longer at home. But he would rather stay where they are. He grew up in this town; he has never lived anywhere else in his life.

The things on the windowsill are Dorothy's. There is a small frame containing an old photograph of a woman. She is so familiar. She has been on the kitchen windowsill for forty years and he has no doubt looked at her every day, and yet he has no idea, he thinks now, who she is. She looks a lot like his Dorothy – perhaps he knew once that it was a favourite aunt or a grandmother, but if he ever knew he doesn't know now.

Next to the photograph is an empty vase, and a stone the

size of his fist. He picks it up, weighs it on his palm. It has a hole worn through the middle; it is like a cored apple. He wonders how it got there, the hole. Through it he can see his own hand, the naked pinkness, his life line and his love line.

Dorothy listens to a programme called *Love Line* on a local radio station. Listeners call in with their own stories about how they met someone or lost someone, with proposals and confessions, and then they request a dedication, a love song. Sentimental popcorn, says Wilfred. He is not one of the world's great romantics, says Dorothy. She used to tease him about calling in with a request for her, but she hasn't mentioned it in a while.

The radio isn't working properly. When he turns it on there is interference, white noise. He picks it up, takes it over to the table and sits down. For a minute, he just holds it, this beautiful, broken old thing, and then he takes a coin out of his pocket, fits it in the slot on top of the plastic case, and twists. The case pops apart.

It is a lovely little transistor radio, a Constant, turquoise and gold. It is the radio Dorothy brought into the antiques shop where he used to work, asking if they did repairs. He wasn't supposed to, said Wilfred, not unless she was selling. He looked at the Vulcan 6T-200 she was holding, her slender thumb with its polished nail toying with the dial. It was foreign; he hadn't seen one before. He didn't know how it worked, what he would find if he prised open the case. But yes, said Wilfred, he could do it.

After they were married, it drove Dorothy mad to find their things in bits all the time – the component parts of the record player all over the carpet, her music box disassembled on the sofa, the mess of stuff all over the kitchen table. She worried about small, crucial pieces getting lost - slipping down behind the sofa cushions, rolling under the fridge, dropping between the floorboards. She told him off for tinkering with things that weren't broken, things that weren't his, for having such busy little fingers.

Dorothy, confined to bed now by her illness, frets about the downstairs rooms she can't see. She imagines Wilfred pottering about dismantling their things; she imagines the dishes and the washing and the dirt piling up. She has to rely on him to keep it all in good order. She says to him, 'All as it should be?'

'All as it should be,' he says, holding out his dishpan hands as proof.

To look at her, he thinks, you wouldn't suspect a thing. You wouldn't know that beneath her clear skin a tumour is eating her alive; you wouldn't know that her calm, grey eyes are going blind. She is losing her memory; she has lost the feeling in her toes. 'When I'm better,' she said, 'we'll go walking again, and I need new walking boots.'

'Yes, love,' he said, taking her dirty cup from the bedside table.

Wilfred sits quietly gutting the radio on the kitchen table, on the plastic tablecloth. The tablecloth depicts the changing seasons. Tiny screws lie at the base of the autumn tree like strange windfall. His right arm rests on winter, the thinning elbow of his cardigan pressing against the bare tree, against the snow, against the cold plastic.

When Dorothy got ill, he didn't change the channel; he

listened to her programme while he washed up, and caught himself singing 'Just One Smile' while he dried the dishes. But mostly he moves about in silence, in socks on the carpet, while Dorothy sleeps upstairs. He feels like a stealthy burglar, quietly rooting through drawers, looking for everyday things which Dorothy has always been in charge of, looking for paper on which to write a letter to his brother-in-law, looking for her recipes so that he can make Dorothy her favourite dessert. He has never written to his brother-in-law or made a dessert in his life; these things are in Dorothy's domain. He feels like a trespasser in Dorothy's house, going through a stranger's things.

He found her scrapbook of favourite recipes in the big bottom drawer in the kitchen, with annotations in pencil – *nice cold the next day, tinned is fine, good with almonds*. Her favourite dessert is tiramisu; it is the first thing she ever made for him. The pencilled note says, *Wilfred didn't like it*.

She is very tidy, Dorothy, but she is a hoarder. In the same drawer, he found a serviette from a café, a handful of seashells, old theatre and concert programmes, a small fluffy toy he once won at a fairground – a cheap thing which she has kept all this time. He found birthday cards – *To Dorothy*, they said each year, *with love from Wilfred* – and the cursory postcards he sent her when he was away from the family on business trips, and half a dozen letters, aged and faded, the postmarks almost as old as their youngest daughter. He took them out and read them and it was like falling through a hole. *My darling*, they said to Dorothy, who was still so young. He leaned his weight on the kitchen counter, the pages quivering from the slight tremble in his fingers. *I love you*, they said, and *Yours always*. He is not, Dorothy has said, an emotional man, but, reading these old letters he found that his cheeks had become wet. He dried them on his shirt sleeve and then pulled the arm of his cardigan down over the damp cuff. He put the letters back in their envelopes and returned them to the drawer. He put everything back the way it had been, keeping it all in good order.

He bends over the radio's innards like a surgeon exploring a patient on the operating table, searching for the fault – looking for something loose, looking for degradation – wanting to fix it; trying, with his set of tiny screwdrivers and his Brasso, to turn back time, to make this old thing like new, as it used to be, as it is supposed to be.

There has never been another woman in his life. He has never wanted anyone but Dorothy.

They honeymooned in Morecambe. They walked on the beach, Dorothy pausing every few steps to pick up some pretty thing which caught her eye, filling her pockets with empty shells. Wilfred, dawdling beside her, wanted nothing more, wanted nothing to change.

They spent their summer holidays in Morecambe too – every year except one, when Dorothy suggested trying somewhere new. They tried Scarborough, but Wilfred didn't enjoy it. 'It's not Morecambe,' he said.

The last of the winter light dribbles in through the two small kitchen windows. The outside world, with all its people, all its noise, all its growth and change, seems miles away. The world is these two windows, these two patches of blank, grey sky. It is not even four o'clock but it is getting dark. He switches on the too-bright striplight which Dorothy would be glad to see the back of, along with the rest of the tired old kitchen. Some of the cupboard doors are loose, and the big bottom drawer sticks, and the sink leaks, and the linoleum floor is worse for wear. 'When I'm better,' Dorothy said, 'we should get a new kitchen – new units, and a sink with a mixer tap, and nice stone tiles on the floor.' A stone floor would be cold in the winter, he said, and mixer taps were unhygienic. He liked it, he said, the way it was, but he would tighten the hinges on the cupboard doors and reseal the sink.

It has been this way for forty years, and it has been just fine, he thinks, so why go making trouble now, why go making all that mess? Has she even looked in that drawer, he wonders – the drawer in which she keeps the recipes she now makes from memory, and the forty-year-old keepsakes, and the faded love letters – in all that time?

And it is just as long since he last took the back off the radio. It has lasted remarkably well. It is simple to fix, as it happens: one deft turn and it is mended; a good clean and polish with a soft cloth and it is restored to its former glory. He puts the two halves of the case together again, snaps them shut, and tests it. It is as good as new. It looks the way it looked when Dorothy returned to the shop at the end of the week, stepping through the doorway and walking towards the counter, her heels loud on the bare floorboards. It looks the way it looked as she turned it over in her hands, admiring his work, as she turned the dial through the stations, found Gene Pitney and lingered there, asking what time he finished work.

He puts on the kettle and rinses out the Duchess teacup.

They went to a café and had a pot of tea. He had a scone

and Dorothy had a tiramisu. Sinking the prongs of her fork into her dessert, she said, 'Italian cakes . . .' and as her lips closed over the first bite, her face said *exquisite*. Between mouthfuls, licking her lips, she said, 'I'd love to go to Italy.'

He puts the radio under his arm and goes upstairs, climbing slowly to keep the tea steady in its cup, his socks deathly quiet on the stair carpet. He opens the bedroom door and puts the tea down on Dorothy's bedside table.

'When you write to my brother,' she says, 'tell him we'll come and visit in the summer.'

'I was thinking,' he says, 'about making your tiramisu.'

Dorothy smiles. 'It's a nice thought, Wilfred,' she says, 'but I'm not sure I have the appetite for it, and you'd just make a mess. And anyway, I don't think I have the recipe any more.'

He watches her, trying to see in her unfocused eyes, in her unchanged expression, whether she has forgotten all these things she has kept in the big bottom drawer which sticks, but he can't tell.

'All as it should be?' she asks him.

He reaches out with a dishpan hand and cups the side of her head, her skull and her warmth in the palm of his hand, his thumb stroking her temple. He takes the radio from under his arm, turns it on and tunes it to Dorothy's favourite station. She smiles. 'All as it should be,' he says.

'When I'm better,' says Dorothy, 'we should go on a proper holiday. I've always wanted to see Italy.'

Wilfred sits down on the edge of the bed, picks up the teacup and puts it in Dorothy's waiting hands. 'Yes,' he says, but the romance countries don't appeal to him.

'This is the wonderful Gene Pitney,' says the DJ, 'with a

song from 1967, for a very special lady.' Dorothy turns her head towards the radio. The DJ says, 'Fiona, this is for you.' She looks away, her failing eyesight sliding over Wilfred's face. She smiles again, and lifts the teacup towards her mouth. 'You're not one of the world's great romantics,' she says, finding the rim, touching her lips to what is left of the gilt.

He has never wanted anyone but Dorothy. But he has never asked for her favourite song to be played on the radio. He has never taken her to Italy. He is not the sort of man who brings home flowers. And he has never written a love letter in his life.

Sometimes You Think You Are Alone

A S SOON AS you wake up, you want to run. Your body craves the endorphins, the endogenous morphine. They experimented on mice, making them want to run and then taking their treadmill away. When they looked at what this did to the mice, to their brains, they found that the mice were suffering from the same symptoms as an addict withdrawing from drugs.

You leave your house at dawn. You run while the streetlamps are still lit, and the odd car which goes by has its headlights on. You run in the same top you slept in, with something fluorescent over it to keep you safe. Most of the houses past which you run are still in darkness. The occasional light goes on behind a still-drawn curtain or blind. The milkman might have begun his rounds but as soon as you can you turn off the road and get onto the dirt track. It is possible that no one at all will see you go by.

You run the same route every day, in all weathers. You know how it feels to run when the ground is hard – dry and dusty or frozen over. You know how it feels to run in the rain, when the dirt track is slippery and the potholes have become puddles and you return home mud-spattered and sodden. You must know every inch of it by now. You could probably run the course blindfolded.

On either side of the dirt track, there are fields. Sometimes there are cows which watch you go by, and sometimes they don't bother looking up. Sometimes there are sheep, and sometimes there's just fleece caught on the barbed wire fence.

While you run, you listen to music, always the same C60 tape, a compilation your boyfriend made for you, before he left you. The first side of the tape takes you as far as the woods.

You can see the woods from the back of your house, the dark shape of them in the distance. In the evening, you sometimes come to your bedroom window to watch the sun go down behind the trees.

As you enter the woods, you turn the tape over and listen to the B-side. By this time you are high on the endorphins, oploids preventing pain signals from reaching the brain. It is the endorphins which keep you running when you would think that you no longer could. You pass the warden's lodge, and the rhododendron bushes in which children make dens. You skirt one end of the old quarry, nearing the bird hides and taking the path which leads you back onto the dirt track, where your tape runs out again.

At the end of the track, the point at which you turned off the road, you stop, exhausted, breathing hard. You must stretch your muscles so as to avoid pain later.

You have come to expect to see a man who walks his dog there before breakfast. At first the two of you were just on nodding terms, but then you began to remove your earphones and say hello to him. You found that both the man and his dog were friendly. Now the man asks after your mother while you pet his dog.

By the time you are back on the road, walking home, it is light and people are up and about. You see them coming out onto their doorsteps in their dressing gowns, fetching in milk, or already dressed for work, going to their cars. You don't know their names and they don't know yours. They are your neighbours but you have never spoken to any of them.

When you get inside your house, you go for a shower. You stand under the shower for a long time. You use products which you think are animal friendly. You don't spend long in front of the mirror or getting dressed. You wear the same outfit for days, thinking no one notices.

You skip breakfast, even though you must be hungry. You must feel hungry most of the time. You don't even have coffee.

You go to work on the bus because you can't drive. You work in an office in town, in an ugly building. I forget what you do there. It is nothing important.

At lunchtime, you sit in the park and feed your sandwiches to the pigeons. You read a book. You always have a book in your bag. You read while you're waiting at the bus stop and on the bus so that no one will talk to you. 'You're never alone with a book,' you say, but you are.

In the evenings, you tend to stay in. You watch a lot of television – you like talent shows. You have an insatiable appetite for show tunes. You used to sing but your father discouraged you. Now your father is dead and you have toyed with the idea of entering one of these contests, but you never have.

You eat a bowl of cereal in front of the television. You like the sugary sort they make for children, with cartoon characters on the packet. You eat a lot of cereal, and cheese. You will try different sorts of cheese but you prefer cheddar. You ought to eat more fruit, and red meat.

You go to bed early so that you can get up as soon as it is light and go running in the woods. Sometimes it takes you a while to get to sleep though, and sometimes you wake with a start in the middle of the night. You have bad dreams.

When you open your eyes, it will be dark. You will try to move your head but it will hurt.

You don't go out much. You rarely drink because you don't want a hangover and you don't care for the taste of alcohol anyway. But because you don't drink often, when you do it really hurts.

On your rare evenings out, with people you think of as your friends, you go to bars where you are given telephone numbers which you won't call.

It is a long time since your boyfriend left but you have been slow to move on. He wasn't right for you but you have trouble seeing it.

You always read the lonely hearts ads in the local paper. You read them all – the women seeking men and women, the men seeking women and men – but you've never answered one.

But last night you went out and you weren't with a friend. For the first time in years, you were out on a date. You went to a restaurant you'd never been to before. You arrived five minutes early and found a bottle of wine already open on the table, waiting for you.

'It's been breathing,' I said, filling your glass.

'I've never tried rosé,' you said, reading the label before taking a sip. You said something complimentary, something banal. You straightened your cutlery and every little thing on the table. You said, 'I never go on dates.'

I noticed that you had plucked your eyebrows. You'd

dressed smartly but your outfit was one you wear for work. It was nothing special and I was disappointed in you.

While we were talking, you kept looking elsewhere, at the staff and at the other customers and at the door. I found it rude. You weren't always paying attention to what I was saying.

It seemed to me that you did not like the wine but you said that you did, and you accepted another glass.

When you drink, you don't get up as soon as it is light and go running, and then you regret it.

When you open your eyes and find that you can barely move, you will have to remember what has happened.

Sometimes, when you wake with a start before it is light, you wonder if you heard something; you think that maybe something you heard woke you up. You listen, considering the possibility that there is someone else in the house. You don't get up to look though; you don't even turn on the light. Sometimes you hear nothing and go back to sleep. Sometimes you hear the garden gate banging and you think, 'It was only the gate.' You don't care that your gate is wide open. You keep your front door locked but you don't always secure your back door. You go to bed leaving windows ajar. You are lazy like that. Or, sitting up in bed, listening to the night, you hear a dog barking. 'It was just a dog,' you think, and you turn over, pulling your double duvet up over your shoulder and closing your eyes again. 'It's all that cheese,' you think, and you go back to sleep.

'It must be all the cheese!' you said, cutting a wedge of

cheddar to put on a digestive biscuit. 'I eat way too much cheese!' You were laughing about how much you like cheese, laughing at yourself telling me that you eat too much cheese even as you were cutting yourself some more, but it wasn't really funny. You laugh a lot, but you're not a funny person. You have an irritating, nervous laugh.

You declined coffee, telling me that you avoid caffeine because it is basically a drug, and then you picked up your wine glass, so that was quite funny.

When you open your eyes, you might feel sick. You will probably be thirsty. You will be cold. This is normal.

As I helped you into your coat, you talked about your father, who never liked your boyfriend or your having a boyfriend at all. Now this boyfriend has left you and your father is dead anyway.

Sometimes you think you are alone, but you are not.

You told me how you felt numb when your father died, and I understand. People experience pain in different ways. Some feel pain right away while for others it comes later, after the initial shock.

When you open your eyes and remember what has happened, you will wish that you had not been out drinking. You will want it to be dawn and to be running in the woods.

I only had one glass of rosé, which I'd poured for myself before you arrived. I don't drink much alcohol. I like to drive.

You heard me joking with someone as I was getting you

into the car. You tried to say something but your tongue wouldn't work. We were as close to your house as mine but I took us to mine. You were asleep even before we'd set off.

I'm a careful driver but your head kept banging against the side window, and the marks on the side of your neck are from where the strap was cutting into you. You wet yourself but you were sitting on a waterproof sheet which I'd put on the passenger seat just in case.

You stirred when we arrived, while I was getting you out. You tried again to talk – you seemed concerned about having lost one of your shoes. When we got inside, you reacted to the smell.

'It's dog meat,' I said.

I carried you into the living room and put you in a plastic-covered armchair. Your mobile rang in your pocket and you seemed to be trying to lift your hand to take it out, to see who was calling you, but you couldn't.

I've turned your mobile off now. You won't be asleep for much longer but I don't want the phone to be what wakes you.

When you open your eyes, it will be dark. You will wonder where you are. You might hear the dog barking and recognise the sound. You will hear my voice, or at least the sound of my breathing or the smallest of movements. You will know that you are not alone.

A Small Window

VALDA HAS NOT yet had her breakfast. She has not even had a cup of tea. She always used to say to John on waking that she was dying for a cuppa. She had learnt all these wonderful phrases. 'I could kill,' she used to say, for this or that.

But her mother discouraged her from using these 'extravagant expressions'. 'You are not starving,' she would say to Valda. 'You are only hungry.'

Valda has readied her teacup. While the kettle boils, she goes to fetch the laundry to put into the machine. She comes out of the kitchen and goes to the stairs, at the foot of which there is a small, round window through which she can see the sea.

This view was one of her favourite things about the house when she first saw it. She remembers stepping in off the street, the estate agent closing the front door behind her, shutting away the busy road. The hallway was dark, but at the far end she could see a circle of light, and when she reached this window at the back of the house she saw through it the white sky and the grey sea and the stony beach, and the house seemed like the wardrobe through which one reached Narnia.

John had liked the house too, although he had been concerned about its proximity to the sea. He mentioned global warming and rising sea levels. And it had been necessary for Valda to explain to her mother over the phone that their house on the beach was really just at the edge of the beach and that they would not be marooned when the tide came in. 'The sea will not come to our door,' she told her mother, but her mother did not sound convinced.

John lives in a city now, in the Midlands.

Valda looks through this window many times each day. She never opens it though, to hear the pounding of the waves or the sound of the pebbles being drawn away. She doesn't have the key anyway. She doesn't know where all the keys have gone.

There is hardly anyone out there, on the beach. But she could not say, 'It is deserted,' because she can see a dark figure in the distance, someone walking beneath the cliff, coming this way, carrying something under one arm. And she can see a dog. There is a woman who regularly walks her dog along the beach, and who, if she sees Valda through the small window, always waves. Valda squints in the direction of this approaching figure.

It is too early for the holidaymakers, who will not arrive on the beach until midmorning. The lifeguards will appear then too, planting their red and yellow flags so that people will know where to swim; they will know where it is safe.

Valda turns away from the window and climbs the stairs. The laundry basket on the landing is only half full. Before taking it down to the kitchen, she goes into her bedroom to look for anything which might need washing. She can't put in her nightie because she is still wearing it.

She goes into the bathroom and brings out a damp hand towel. On the other side of the bathroom, there is another bedroom, but it is empty. There is no bed in there with covers to straighten or change, no clothes on the floor to pick up, no drawers into which to tidy things away. They were going to paint the walls, but then John left. She has never been sure whether the cartoon people on the wallpaper are deep-sea divers or astronauts. Each one is wearing a helmet, a circular opening or window at the front framing a round face. They are floating on a dark-blue background which could be the sky where it becomes space, or which could be the sea, deep down. They seem stranded, she thinks, but they are smiling.

She carries the laundry basket downstairs and pauses again by the window. She can see now that it is a young boy approaching beneath the cliff, and that what he has with him is a surfboard.

The dog is running into and out of the water and trotting along in the wet sand revealed by the falling tide. Valda thinks about the sand and salt which will cling to its nut-brown coat.

She hears the kettle reaching boiling point. It is hours since she woke up wanting that first cup of tea of the day, but every morning a certain number of chores must be done before she will allow herself to have it.

Taking the laundry basket into the kitchen, she loads the washing machine and sets it going. She watches it for a while, the soapy water rising up behind the glass door, her things sloshing and tumbling. Her family pack of detergent is almost empty. She had a freezer full of food, a cupboard full of provisions, but it is nearly all gone. There is only her and she is careful, but of course it goes in the end.

Lifting the still-steaming kettle, she pours hot water into her cup and fishes out the teabag. She doesn't like it too strong. She adds some long-life milk and is just putting in her sweetener when the telephone rings. Going back out into the hallway, to the phone she keeps on a table in front of the little window, she lifts the receiver to her ear but there is no one there. It is one of those cold calls which leave you standing there saying, 'Hello? Hello?' with no reply.

That young boy is near the water now. He is wearing one of those short wetsuits. He must be cold, thinks Valda. It looks cold out there. But maybe it isn't. She doesn't know. She has not been outside recently. His wetsuit looks, she thinks, like something he has grown out of, like something for which his prepubescent limbs are now too long. She wonders whether it can really keep him warm in the cold water.

He stands at the edge of the sea, with his back to her. Valda looks along the beach, hoping to see someone who will notice the boy and tell him that he shouldn't go out there. But apart from the boy and the dog, she can't see a soul.

The boy begins his walk into the water, holding on to his board. He does not inch out like John used to do, and like she imagines she would except that she does not swim at all. He strides, appearing to have no fear of this grey sea, not to feel its chill. He lies tummy-down on his surfboard and paddles further out to where the sea looks especially rough. Uncertainly, he stands, and is immediately knocked off his board by a wave and Valda loses sight of him. Someone, she thinks, needs to warn him, to stand on the shore and shout, 'You shouldn't be out there!' or, 'It isn't safe!' or, 'Come back!'

She sees him again, his head and shoulders out of the water. He climbs back onto his surfboard, and again he is instantly bowled over. The sea is rough today, full of big waves. She watches until she finds him again, scrambling onto his board. He is trying so hard but he can't seem to stay on his feet.

She puts her hand on the doorknob and then takes it off again. He wouldn't hear her anyway; she would be shouting into the wind. And besides, the door is locked and she can't think where the key might be. She goes back into the kitchen and fetches her tea, carrying it towards the living room. But she diverts once again to the window, peering out. At first, she doesn't see him, and then she does and he is so far out, and still there is no one to tell him that he shouldn't be there. Even the dog is nowhere in sight.

She begins opening drawers: the ones in the telephone table, hunting through scraps of paper and pens; and the ones in which she keeps woolly hats and gloves, searching underneath them, finding pebbles and shells and, right there after all with these other bits and pieces, where it must have been all along, the key for the back door. There is a slight tremble in her hand as she puts the key in the lock and turns it. When she pulls at the door, it sticks and she remembers that the sea air does this to the wood. She has to put all her strength into it and is taken by surprise when the door suddenly opens.

She hurries out over the shingle, down to the shore where the waves crash down before sliding back out, dragging the smaller stones with them.

Taking no care to keep her slippers dry, she stands in the shallows and yells to the boy in the sea, 'You shouldn't be out there!' She wades out with only her nightclothes to protect her from the cold. She can feel the current tugging at her bare legs. She is astonished by the power of the waves which topple her and return her to the beach, the sea spitting her out like unwanted gristle.

Someone says, 'Are you all right?'

Valda looks up. The woman who waves is standing above her, the nut-brown dog beside her. Valda, on her knees now in the surf, in her sodden nightie, tries to tell the woman about the boy. 'He's too far out,' she says.

'He's OK,' says the woman. 'Let me help you.' She takes one of Valda's hands and gets her onto her feet. 'You're freezing,' she says.

Valda remembers the tea which she has not yet had. It is still on the sill beneath the small window and will need heating through. Or she might need to make a fresh pot for this woman who is probably going to come inside her house, who is walking beside her now, over the stones to her back door. The three of them – Valda and the woman and the dog – are going to walk the beach right into the house. There will be paw prints in the hallway. The house will smell of wet dog and the sea long after the woman and her dog have gone home. Valda will keep finding sand.

When they reach the back door, Valda, turning, sees the lifeguards arriving. She watches them carrying their red and yellow flags onto the beach, planting them in the pebbles, putting one on either side of the stretch of sea in which the boy is surfing, marking out a zone which they will patrol. She turns back to the house and opens the door and the dog goes in first.

The Smell of the Slaughterhouse

RACHEL'S FATHER OPENS the door and looks at her. Seeing her small suitcase, he says, 'Is that it?'

'I'll go back for more,' she says. She will go when Stan's out. If she goes when he's in, he will tell her that he loves her, and she doesn't want to hear it. Or perhaps she won't go back. She could leave it all behind and buy new clothes, new everything.

Stepping inside, she sees that she is treading something into the house. She leaves the offending shoe outside, puts the other one on the shoe rack and hangs up her coat. Her father, closing the door behind her, fetches paper towels and carpet freshener. Then he picks up her suitcase and she follows him through the floral mist to the stairs.

He carries her suitcase up to her room, puts it down on the bed and says, 'I'll leave you to it.'

She packed hastily but has remembered her make-up. She takes her cosmetics case into the bathroom, where she washes her hands and face with her father's soap before reapplying her foundation, covering the bruising.

Back in her bedroom, she undresses, putting her clothes into the laundry basket and choosing something clean from her suitcase. She puts the rest of her things into the drawers and onto hangers. Her room has not changed at all. When she has finished unpacking and has put her empty suitcase under the bed, it is almost as if she has never been away.

She can hear the kettle boiling and crockery chinking in the kitchen.

Downstairs, she finds her father on his way into the dining room with a pot of tea, cups and a packet of lemon sponge fingers on a tray. Putting everything down on the table, he says, 'Shall I be mother?'

Her mother always had a clean shirt waiting for Rachel's father when he got in from work, ready for him to put on after his shower. He smelt heavily of his carbolic soap at teatime.

There was always a cloth on the dining table, and something home-baked. There might be some quiet jazz on the stereo. Her mother would pour the tea and ask about his day. He never really talked about it though. 'Fine,' he would say, or, 'Busy.'

Her mother would say, 'Good,' or, 'It's better to be busy,' and nothing much more would be said.

Rachel, sitting down now at the table and accepting sugar in her tea, remembers how she used to look at her father, at the well-washed hands in which he held his slice of cake and his teacup, and she would think to herself that no one would know he had just come from the abattoir.

Except that the smell of the carbolic soap with which he scrubbed himself daily, and whose reek is on her own skin now, has come to seem to her, over the years, like the smell of the slaughterhouse itself.

Helicopter Jean

'NOW THEN,' SAYS my father, pushing the nettles aside with the umbrella, 'which way?' We consider our choice of muddy paths. 'I think we'll try down there,' he says, and we walk on, completely lost. 'Did we come this way before?' he asks. 'Did we turn left or right here?'

'I don't know,' I say. 'Maybe left.' I don't recognise it at all. Left looks drier.

'Left it is,' he says.

He is wearing his windcheater, the same one he wore for Sunday walks when I was small. He is carrying my mother's umbrella. It is pastel-coloured and patterned with tiny flowers and has a wrist loop which he has utilised.

He points the umbrella at a stream and says, 'That shouldn't be here, that should be way over there.' He frowns down at the stream, annoyed. 'All right,' he says, 'we'll try this way,' and we push on.

We came here often in my childhood. I should know it better than this. I recognise the smell of the bracken, and dung from the nearby farm. I remember the tall, thin trees with high, sparse branches, and the bluebells. I remember riding on my father's shoulders with my head seven feet in the air, his hands around my ankles, my mother striding ahead singing hymns and 'Leaving on a Jet Plane'. She was the only one with any sense of direction. She had an aerial view in her head and was our guide. She could stand in the middle of the woods and point north or north-north-east or to home. It is a skill I did not inherit.

'This is right,' he says, hopefully. We pass a horse chestnut tree and he stops and pokes at the lower branches with the umbrella. He says, 'Do you remember being lost on Blankenberge beach?'

'Yes,' I say, 'I do.'

I had stayed with my mother, sitting between two breakwaters, while my father went to the pier. I watched him walk away down the beach, becoming a tiny figure in the distance, and then decided I wanted to go too. Leaving my mother sunbathing, I followed him, or tried to. I lost him for a while and then spotted him on the pier. I shouted but he was too far away to hear me. I couldn't see how to get up there. There must have been steps in the wall somewhere but I couldn't for the life of me find them. So I walked back towards where I had left my mother but I couldn't find her either. I had no landmarks other than the breakwaters and they all looked the same. I went to and fro, back to the pier which I could not reach and then back to the breakwaters, walking further and further up the beach until finally I saw her, sitting in the shade in her turquoise swimsuit, just her feet in the sun. But when I arrived, when she looked up, it was a stranger's face which smiled at me.

In fact, my mother wasn't there, where I was looking. She had packed up and gone to the pier. She was already up there, high above the beach. But I didn't know this at the time. I felt very lost and wondered what would happen if I never found them again. In my head, I practised saying No to strange men.

'When we realised you weren't with either of us,' says my

father, 'I left your mother on the pier and came to look for you. I could see you on the beach. You were a long way off, walking towards me. I stood and watched you. You looked very serious.'

Turning and walking back towards the pier, I was surprised to find just how far I had wandered, how far from the pier I was. And I was still looking for a distant figure, concentrating on the place where I had last seen my father. I didn't see him standing right there on the promenade, watching me.

'You would have been about eight,' he says.

When I was about eight, my father used to sit at the kitchen table, topping and tailing the green beans he had grown in the garden. He worked very quietly and precisely, cutting neat diagonals until he had a bowl full of parallelograms which my mother boiled. He was cool with a kitchen knife. He could peel a cooking apple in one long curl of green skin, and I watched him with eyes which were his, only smaller.

I was about eight in the days of Beautiful Jean, ballroom dancing on a Monday night, my mother coming downstairs in a sexy, floaty dress like Angela Rippon on *Morecambe and Wise*, and my father standing at the foot of the stairs watching her, saying, 'Beautiful Jean,' as he held out his arm for her to take. Then one week he said instead, 'Shall we give it a miss? I think we're a bit past dancing, don't you?' She stood on the stairs and grew old then and there. Her waist expanded and her feet grew corns, and she turned and went back upstairs, her sequins catching the light before she disappeared.

I entered adolescence. My father, troubled by his overgrown daughter, by the sudden appearance of a young woman where his little girl had been, became the slowly turning pages of a newspaper and the opening and closing of the lounge door while I sat in front of the television watching *Blake's Seven*, in which Surrey was an alien planet.

Meanwhile, my mother was cutting the beans herself, or bringing them to me and telling me not to fuss with them, just to cut them, they were just beans. She went walking on her own, wearing his windcheater.

One Saturday, somebody phoned and spoke to my father, who came upstairs to my bedroom, knocking on my closed door, to tell me that my mother had fallen and broken her ankle. After being found by another walker, she'd been helicoptered to the hospital. My father went to see her, leaving me at a neighbour's house.

Mrs Abbott let me into her kitchen. It was a nice kitchen – spotless, not a thing out of place. There was a crystal bowl of pristine fruit on the side and the bin was in a cupboard. It looked like a show-home or studio-set version of our own. She sat me down at the kitchen table and then stood back and looked at me, as if she might decide I looked untidy there and put me somewhere else. She smiled pleasantly and said, 'Your poor father. Your mother's always had a *streak* in her, hasn't she?'

I asked to use the loo. 'I know where it is,' I said, the house being exactly like ours.

Upstairs, all the doors were closed. I opened the door to my right and stood there, unsettled to find that this was not the bathroom. Where we had our bathroom, the Abbotts had their main bedroom, and lounging on the rumpled bed was Mr Abbott wearing nothing but his socks, smoking a cigarette. Wagging a hairy leg to and fro, he said, 'Coming in?' Then he laughed and shrugged and said, 'Only joking. Toilet? Next one along.'

I closed the bedroom door.

In the Abbotts' immaculate bathroom, I used the loo. While I sat there, I leafed through Mrs Abbott's magazines. When I was finished, I looked for toilet paper but couldn't see any, so I used the magazines, tearing pages from *The Lady* and *Beautiful Home*. Then I went back downstairs.

I visited Mum in hospital and one nurse said to another, 'This is Jean's daughter.'

'Which Jean?'

'Helicopter Jean.'

I loved Helicopter Jean. I pictured her flying high above the treetops, becoming a dot in the distance, a speck in the sky, the helicopter glinting in the sunlight.

For a while, my father called her Helicopter Jean and it made them both smile.

A conker falls. 'That's a beauty,' he says, polishing and pocketing it, pleased. He is like a boy with a champion conker, for whom Beautiful Jean is still in the future, shimmering like a mirage, waiting to be wooed and won.

We have gone wrong somewhere. We don't recognise this bare clearing. We retrace our steps. He starts to hum, to peck at her songs, but he doesn't know the words. 'Heavens above . . .' he says. 'Heavens above . . .'

The cancer was like a rat in a pantry, creeping in during the night and spoiling her eyesight, her muscles, her memory.

Beautiful Jean, lying downstairs on a medical bed, tried to

remember her hymns. 'Heaven above . . . Heaven above below below . . . Heaven above . . . Hello?'

'Hello,' said my father. 'Hello, love, we're here.'

'Hello?' said my mother again. 'Can I come in? How do I get into the box?'

She could barely see us now. We watched her, our eyes gleaming, wondering where she was.

'It's all over,' said my father, later, in the kitchen, bypassing this dying, hurrying out of this jungle and into a bleak place.

When my mother died, my father and I found ourselves standing in what had once been our dining room, surrounded by swabs and pads, plastic sheets and plastic mugs, talking books and wigs. We returned these things to the hospice and the library and tried to remember where we had been before.

I found memories of her secreted in unexpected places: in the bathroom cabinet which smelt of her face soap when I went looking for spare toothpaste, and in the darkness of her wardrobe where her scent lingered on her abandoned clothes. When I found her, I stood still and inhaled, time-travelling.

I took my mother's ashes to the woods when the bluebells were thick. I trudged along behind my father, wondering which way to go now that nobody here had a map in their head. He carried the pot of ashes like a priest with an incense burner, his old windcheater for a cassock. He tried to sing 'Leaving on a Jet Plane' but he only knew the first two lines.

We scattered her ashes around a sycamore tree which was almost in the sun. It seemed as if something momentous ought to happen, but the ashes just fell to the ground, onto the grass and onto our shoes.

There was some graffiti carved into the bark of the tree, near the base.

My father traced its lines and said, 'What does this mean?'

I told him: 'True Love For Ever' and 'If Destroyed Still True'.

To our right, the woods gave way to a field full of drowsy cows, and beyond it a busy road roared with traffic. We walked back the way we had come, the pot empty in my father's hands, something precious left behind, just out of reach of the sun.

I drifted back to my flat, my boyfriend and my job, and my father is growing green beans again, eating parallelograms for tea. He phones me to ask, 'How long for potatoes?' and how hot a towel wash should be. He asks me if I eat vegetables and how often I clean my floors. We are beginning carefully, getting our bearings.

In my father's memories, I am forever eight years old, a time-traveller in a Tom Baker *Doctor Who* scarf. He is bewildered if I say that I was not, on this or that occasion, eight but thirteen or fourteen years old. I crash around inside him, vandalising his memories, stealing his eight-year-old girl.

I tell him about my first and secret boyfriend and he tells me about his brief engagement to a girl before Mum. I tell him about the two times I've been in hospital having stitches and never said and he tells me about the time he almost died skidding on a motorbike on black ice across oncoming traffic.

❧

It was spring when we last stood here. Now it is autumn. Trees which were green are now bare and the paths are buried beneath the leaves. The bluebells are gone and the wood feels empty despite the evergreens – holly hurrying us into winter, like Christmas menus appearing in pubs on the first of September. The holly must have been here before, with the bluebells, but I didn't notice it then, in the spring.

Neither my father nor I can find our way to the place where we left Jean. Her umbrella swings at his side like a pendulum, and he says, 'Which way? Left or right? Was this fallen tree here before? I think I remember this, don't you?' We are in a clearing where many paths meet, and I do remember this but I don't know which way to go. 'Is it this one, do you think?' he says and I randomly agree. We take a path.

The violence of it burns our eyes. The stink of petrol hangs thick in the air. To our right is an empty field, and beyond it, a busy road. Fingers of sunlight stretch towards the stump of a tree, falling just short of the initials I.D.S.T., the only part of the message left in the bark of the sycamore amputee. In front of the stump is a burnt-out car, its body a carcass of battered rust, its bonnet off, its engine exposed, its windows smashed and its doors ripped off, its back seat stripped and empty beer cans resting on the springs.

'Good God,' says my father, staring, trying to make sense of it. He puts his hands in the pockets of his windcheater, where they will curl around the contents – assorted tissues, mints – and he will remember that Jean was the last one to wear it.

My father, with a pocketful of treasure, fishes out the sweets and says, 'Polo?'

We suck at our mints with a hole in the middle. We circle the car as if it is an art installation we would like to understand. My father says, 'Someone's gone to a lot of trouble.'

Something glints, catching my eye, and I look up, as if I might see Helicopter Jean flying high above the treetops, high above the field and the road and all the traffic, singing 'Leaving on a Jet Plane' as she goes.

Small Animals

'WHERE ARE WE?' asked Heather, waking up, sitting forward a little in her seat to peer through the windscreen. She had fallen asleep in the last of the daylight, and now it was dark. On one side of the winding, unmarked road, there was a vertical wall of rock, and on the other, a drop. There were no pavements, no streetlights. There was no moon.

'We're almost there,' said Marilyn, and as she spoke they rounded a bend and Heather saw a house built into the hillside, lit suddenly by the full beam of their headlights. Marilyn slowed and pulled onto the patch of tarmac beside the house, killing the engine, killing the lights. They sat for a moment in silence, looking at the house, at its dark windows.

'Have we got the right night?' said Heather. Marilyn was the one who knew Kath and who had arranged the evening, inviting Heather to join them for dinner and offering to drive. Something about it had seemed a bit odd and Heather suspected something, perhaps matchmaking – a man would be sprung on her at the last minute. This had happened before to Heather, who was unmarried, unattached, and retired now from her life as a teacher and child psychologist. There had been some uneasy dinner parties, some disastrous occasions, in her time.

Marilyn had said to Heather, 'You must meet Kath,' and she had described the unusual house in which Kath lived. Heather, with nothing to do on a Friday night, and struck by the image of this house set into the rocks, had accepted the invitation.

'There's no car here,' said Heather. There was no space, anyway, for another car on the tarmac, and there was no garage. 'Does that mean she's out?'

'She doesn't drive,' said Marilyn, opening the car door.

Heather, who lived in a small town, gazed out at the unlit night. She had never seen such darkness. 'Imagine,' she said, 'being this far from civilization with no transport.' But Marilyn was out of the car now and Heather was talking to herself.

Marilyn rang the doorbell. They heard it, faintly, chiming in the hallway. They waited but no light came on behind the panel of glass above the solid wooden door. Marilyn knocked, but she had her gloves on and the sound was muffled. She took them off, exposing her fingers to the icy night air, rapping her bared knuckles sharply against the door.

Heather walked around to the back of the house and saw windows which were narrow, arched at the top, coming to a point, making her think of a castle. She saw an upstairs light snap off behind drawn curtains. Returning to the porch, she mentioned this to Marilyn. She said, 'There's someone in.'

Marilyn reached for the door handle and turned it, finding the door unlocked. She stuck her head into the dark hallway and called, 'Hello?'

They both heard the creak of floorboards coming from inside, upstairs. Looking up, they saw the shape of someone on the landing, but still some seconds passed before the shape moved onto the top step and the hallway light went on and there was a woman, thin and pale, descending the stairs saying, 'Marilyn, what are you doing here?'

﹡

'I've not got much in,' said Kath, switching on the lamps. 'Sit down.' Taking off their coats, laying them over the arms of the sofa, they sat. Heather noted the anxiety with which Kath glanced around her living room, which looked tidy enough to Heather. 'I'll go and have a look in the kitchen.'

When Kath was out of the room, Heather said to Marilyn, 'What's going on? Has she forgotten we were coming?'

Marilyn shook her head. 'She didn't know.'

'She didn't know we were coming? We weren't invited?'

Kath came in with a bowl of nuts. She pulled the smallest coffee table from a nest and put it in front of her guests.

'Where's Nina?' asked Marilyn.

Kath, placing a doily on the table, the bowl of nuts on the doily, the nutcrackers next to the bowl, said, 'She's sleeping.'

'Is she?' said Marilyn. 'It's early.' And Heather, who had not checked the time when she woke in the car in the dark and had not done so since, was surprised, when she glanced at the carriage clock on Kath's mantelpiece, to find that it was not even six o'clock. It felt later.

Kath returned to the kitchen and Marilyn reached for the nutcrackers and a hazelnut.

'Who's Nina?' asked Heather.

'Nina,' said Marilyn, shattering the nut's thin shell, catching the pieces in her hand and tidying them back into the bowl, 'is Kath's daughter.' She ran her eyes around the room – the walls, the sideboard, the shelves – looking, thought Heather, for a photo, but not finding one. 'She's five,' said Marilyn. 'She's the spit of Kath.'

Kath walked back in with some Tupperware, handing Marilyn a fridge-cold tub of little sandwiches with the crusts cut off. She gave Heather a plate of iced cakes.

'Do you want coffee?' asked Kath. 'Or water?'

Coffee, they said.

'It's instant,' said Kath, going off down the hallway again.

Heather, turning to Marilyn, said, 'What are we doing here? Why did you let me think we'd been invited for dinner, when clearly we haven't?'

'Kath's been avoiding me,' said Marilyn. 'I've been trying to fix up a dinner for months but she's been putting me off.'

'So you drove all the way up here anyway. And what am I doing here?'

'I wanted you to meet her.'

'What if she'd been out?'

'She never goes out.'

There was a rattling of teacups and teaspoons on saucers on a metal tray and the two women turned quickly and smiled at Kath as she entered the room. They cleared the coffee table so that Kath could set down the tray, and then sat with their hands full, unsure what to do with it all.

Heather was pleased at least that Marilyn wasn't drinking, that wine had not been offered. She didn't want this to turn into one of Marilyn's sleepovers. The distance was not remotely walkable and there was no one she could have called, other than a taxi company. But on such occasions in the past, Marilyn had always reminded Heather that there was no one waiting up for her and nowhere she had to be in the morning, and Heather had stayed.

Marilyn said to Kath, 'Can I pop up and see her?'

'Better not,' said Kath.

'I'll be quiet.'

'Best not.' She sugared Marilyn's coffee, knowing how Marilyn took it. She sugared Heather's without asking.

Heather could hear a quiet, persistent beeping sound. When it occurred to her that it was coming from her phone, she put down the cakes and felt around in her coat pockets until she found her phone and a missed message.

'I've got a text from my mother,' she said. 'I'd better reply.'

'You won't get a signal out here,' said Marilyn. 'Is it urgent?'

'It could wait until morning,' said Heather, still holding her phone, still gazing with concern at her mother's message.

'It's an unusual house,' said Heather, offering the cakes to Kath. 'You're very brave.'

Kath, refusing one, said, 'Why?'

'Living so far from town with no transport,' said Heather.

'There are buses,' said Kath.

'They don't run out here at night though,' said Marilyn.

'No,' said Kath, 'they don't.'

While Kath was loading the Tupperware and crockery into the dishwasher, Marilyn said to Heather, 'Nina's a difficult child. She runs away. Someone always brings her home, but it's frightening, she's so young. Kath keeps telling her she mustn't do it, that one day something bad will happen to her. It's a beautiful spot – you can't tell in the dark but in daylight there's a breathtaking view – but it's dangerous. There's a steep drop down to the river, and the traffic goes so fast on the road. There was a flasher once – that was years ago, but still. And it's only months since a local girl went missing.

'She makes nuisance calls to strangers and taxi companies. There have been acts of vandalism. I'm astonished actually,' she said, 'to see nothing damaged. There's usually a broken window or mirror or picture frame, crayon on the walls.'

So, thought Heather, Marilyn had invited her here to observe the child, to offer a professional judgement. Could she not have been told that? She might have come anyway.

'Kath finds mice laid out on her doorstep, and other small animals, dead ones, or as good as dead.'

'The work of a cat, surely?' said Heather.

'They don't have a cat.'

'A neighbour's cat?'

'They don't have neighbours, not for miles. And besides, these mice have not been killed by a cat.'

'Is it necessarily Nina though?' asked Heather.

'Well,' said Marilyn, 'that's another thing. Nina says it isn't her; she says it's another little girl who breaks things, makes these telephone calls, kills the mice. Kath had another little girl, before Nina, but she died. Nina says it's her.'

'You think it's a ghost?'

'No,' said Marilyn, 'it's definitely Nina. But *she* blames a ghost. She often wakes up screaming in the middle of the night.'

'They sometimes do,' said Heather, 'at this age. They have night terrors.'

'She wakes up bruised.'

Heather, standing, said to Kath, 'May I use your bathroom?'

Kath looked at her for a moment, as Heather had once

looked at schoolchildren when they raised their hands and requested the freedom of the empty corridors, before nodding.

'Up the stairs,' said Kath, 'and straight ahead. Straight ahead,' she repeated as Heather left the room, 'when you get to the top.'

The hallway light was off again and Heather climbed the stairs in the dark. Holding her hands out in front of her, in front of her face and her chest, she found the bathroom door. She opened it, feeling for the pull cord, the light.

Looking in the mirror over the sink while washing her hands, she noticed the Rawlplug-stuffed screw holes around it, a different shade of paint, the shape of another mirror which had once hung there.

Leaving the bathroom, she saw that she was outside a room on whose door brightly coloured letters spelled out 'NINA'. The door was slightly ajar, the light from the bathroom spilling into the room, and Heather, pushing the door further open, saw the little girl in her bed, the head of blond hair which was indeed like Kath's. She regarded the room, a lovely one, with crayoned pictures on the walls, books on the shelves, an animal theme on the borders and curtains, and teddies by the girl's pillow, watching over her while she slept. She realised that this was the room she had seen from outside, whose light she had seen go out.

She went in, leaving the door standing open for the illumination. She stood by Nina's bed, looking down at this five-year-old girl who looked quite peaceful. She looked around. She could see nothing torn or broken in the room. Turning back to the bed, she lifted, very carefully, one side of the duvet, looking at the girl's arm, which was bare beneath her cap sleeve. She inspected the other side too. She moved to the foot of the bed and peeled back the bottom of the duvet, peering at her legs, her shins. There were bruises, but children did get bruises. Heather wasn't sure that there was anything unusual. Covering the child up again, Heather retreated to the door. Before she closed it she glanced back, her heart leaping into her throat when she saw that the girl's eyes were wide open, that she was watching her go.

She had just returned to her place on the sofa when the front door opened. Even in the living room, they felt the cold coming in from outside. They heard a man's voice hissing, 'Who the fuck is here? Whose fucking car is that?' They heard the whisper of Kath's reply but not the words. 'They've parked in my fucking space,' said the man. 'I've had to park on the fucking road. Some fucker's going to crash into me.'

Heather turned to Marilyn. They were alone in the room but still Heather mouthed her question silently: *Who's that?*

Marilyn shook her head, widened her eyes, shrugged, as the man strode into the living room and stood in front of them with a takeaway pizza box in his hands.

'Have you had a nice evening?' he said. 'Have you had a nice dinner?'

He turned his head sharply away from them then, towards the door he'd just come through. Putting down his pizza box, he marched back into the unlit hallway. Heather saw the little girl crouching on the stairs in her nightie. The man put his foot on the bottom step. 'Get up,' he said, through his teeth, 'the fucking stairs.' And then they went, this man and this girl, up the stairs, observed by Heather and Marilyn.

Heather, creeping back into the hallway, saw that Kath had vanished. There was a smell of urine, which reminded her of her mother's residential home, although they masked it there. She pictured her mother sitting alone in her bedroom, or in her armchair in the lounge, watching the local news on the television with the sound turned down, clutching the mobile phone which Heather had given her. It frightened her mother, this mobile phone. 'But,' Heather had said, 'now you can text me and I'll text you or call you right back.'

Going into the kitchen, finding Kath, she said, 'Would you mind if I just used your phone?' It was there on the wall between them, its tangled cord hanging down.

'We had it disconnected,' said Kath. And Heather recalled the mention of prank phone calls, and the taxi companies which presumably no longer bothered to come to the house.

There was heavy footfall on the stairs and the man came into the kitchen, glowering at both of them.

'We should go,' said Heather. 'Then you can get your car off the road.' She returned to the living room and said again, to Marilyn, 'We should go.' Usually, she would have added, 'It's getting late,' but it was not.

Marilyn was already on her feet, had made a move towards the door to the hallway, but was now standing still. She seemed frozen.

'What's wrong?' said Heather.

'I'm just going to—' said Marilyn, and she made her way into the hallway, pausing on the stairs before climbing slowly up towards the bathroom, leaving her sentence dangling.

Heather waited alone in the living room, picking up her coat and putting it on, picking up Marilyn's coat, picking up their bags. When Marilyn came down the stairs again, Heather met her in the living room doorway, smelling again the urine in the carpet.

Marilyn spoke, but so quietly that Heather could not hear her.

'What?' she said. She noticed Marilyn's pallor and wondered if she was feeling sick. She began to lead her back into the living room, to sit her down. Marilyn was resisting, opening her mouth to say more, but at that moment there came from outside the sound of an explosion of glass.

Heather hurried to the window and peered out but she had a poor view.

'Is it his car?' said Marilyn. 'Has there been an accident?'

Heather, with her face close to the cold pane, looking at the broken driver's side window and the glass on the ground, said, 'No, it's yours.'

She was looking for Nina, who must have got out of her bed and squeezed her skinny body through those narrow upstairs windows, shinning, she supposed, down a drainpipe or a tree so as to throw a rock through the window of Marilyn's car. She was worried about the girl, about small, bare feet on all that broken glass. She was worried about her being so close to the dark road. She was worried about her running away in her nightie, about flashers and stories of missing girls. She could not see anyone out there.

Marilyn, still in the doorway, went not to the window but to the front door. She turned the handle but found the door locked. Heather, coming to join her, tried the locked door too.

'It isn't Nina,' said Marilyn.

'How do you know?' She had not been able to see who it

was, from the living room window, through this solid door. She did not see how Marilyn could know that.

There was a sudden din then from outside, a banging of metal on metal. Heather returned to the living room window, staring out again, seeing slashed tyres, seeing clearly now the attack on Marilyn's car, whose bonnet was open, whose engine was being ruined.

'It isn't Nina,' repeated Marilyn.

'No,' said Heather, coming back to stand with Marilyn at the door. 'It's him.'

'I mean,' said Marilyn, 'the girl in Nina's bed. It isn't Nina.'

The dishwasher went on in the kitchen and Heather turned around. Kath was standing at the end of the hallway; and at the top of the stairs, in her bedroom doorway, was the girl who was not Nina – and Heather, in that moment, understood that the windows might be big enough to squeeze through but that they would not open.

They heard the key being turned in the front door lock.

They felt the cold night flooding in.

Trees in the Tarmac

PRETTY MUCH EVERYTHING around here is con-
crete – the secondary school, the pebble-dashed scout hut,
the empty working men's club. Nicola, walking home with her
blazer off, steps over the gaps between the paving slabs, over
the weeds which sprout there.

She is wishing away the remaining weeks of term, looking
forward to the summer holidays. Her granddad says that these
will be the happiest days of her life, but she doubts he knows
what he is talking about. Nicola, who is almost sixteen, won't
be going back to school in the autumn.

Closer to home, the pavements are tarmacked. Every few
metres, there is a tree. The roots have broken through the
tarmac, and grass grows in the cracks. The trees must have
been planted when the street was new but Nicola can't help
thinking of them as something belonging to the land on which
the estate was built. The trees and the grass seem to her like
survivors from the buried fields pushing through.

She is not old enough to remember the estate not being here.
She can barely imagine the absence of these solid brick houses
and the line of shops. The units at either end – not long ago
a grocer's and a newsagent's which became an off-licence and
then a video shop – are standing empty except for the unopened
post, mostly junk mail, collecting behind their front doors. In
between, her granddad's sweet shop remains. Her granddad says
that he is not going anywhere. Besides, this is where they live.

The paint on the window frames of her granddad's shop is a sickly red like the liquorice laces and the cherry lips in the jars on the shelves. When the paint peels, her granddad strips it and then repaints it the same colour.

Each afternoon, when Nicola gets in from school, she helps out in the shop. She has only once failed to go straight home after school and she won't be doing that again.

She goes in through the front. As she opens the door, the bell rings and her granddad looks up from his puzzle book. The locals come in to see her granddad as much as they do to buy sweets. They lean on the counter and chat. The shop is never busy anyway. The primary school used to be nearby and the shop got packed at home time – lots of little hands touching whatever wasn't in a jar, fingering the two pence sweets displayed in a tray on the counter. But that school has been closed down now and the children go by bus to a bigger one near the new supermarket.

Nicola's granddad quizzes her about her day and tells her about his before saying, 'Right then, it's all yours.' He leaves her to mind the shop while he goes for a break, which means a cup of tea and a smoke and maybe a nap in his room.

She does think of it as his room now, as opposed to her grandparents' room, although it is just as it used to be when her grandmother was alive. None of her grandmother's things have been removed. The mystery she had been reading is still by the bed. Her slippers are still on the floor. Her clothes are still in her drawers and on her side of the wardrobe, spilling over to her granddad's side, her dresses pressing up against his good, dark suit.

Nicola's granddad does not allow Nicola to touch her

grandmother's possessions. She does though, while he is sleeping. There are things of her grandmother's which Nicola would like to have. Amongst the clothes in the wardrobe, on a hanger in the dark, there is a dress from the fifties with a busy ivy pattern. It makes Nicola think of the inside of her grand-dad's shed, the ivy growing through the walls and through the roof, through the planks. Nicola covets this dress, and the shoes which go with it. And she would like to be given what her grandmother called her crystal ball but which is really just hollow glass. Her grandmother used her crystal ball to read Nicola's palm, telling her how many children she would have – the first one, she said, a year after marrying.

The late afternoon heat presses up against the window of the sweet shop, warming the glass and showing up all the little finger marks on the panes. Her granddad told her that glass is fluid, that over time a window will thicken at the base, imperceptibly swelling.

Nicola sits down on her granddad's stool, slipping off her shoes, letting them fall to the floor, and undoing the button on the waist of her skirt. She feels tired. She would like to put her head down on the sugar-dusted counter and fall asleep. But the door is opening, the bell ringing, a customer entering. Some people are disappointed if they come in and see Nicola and not her granddad behind the counter, but one or two of them, she thinks, come in to see her. This man is one of her regulars.

He looks for a long time at the wall of jars in the window before choosing something off the top shelf. Today, he asks for liquorice. Nicola discreetly refastens her skirt before going to the front of the shop and climbing onto a step stool, reaching for the jar. She knows he is watching her. She can feel his eyes on her, perhaps on the two inches of knee revealed between the top of her knee-high socks and the hem of her skirt, perhaps on the curve of her stomach exposed when her shirt, which she has not tucked into her waistband, rides up as she lifts her arms. He lets her get the jar in both hands before he says, 'Not those, the other sort.' She puts the jar of liquorice laces back on the shelf, fetches down the one he wants and takes it to the counter. She weighs out his liquorice, pouring a quarter pound of it into the steel tray. It is the colour of black pudding.

She likes the boiled sweets herself. They are like fragments of stained glass through which the sunlight filters, making blue and yellow and raspberry-red puddles on the floor of the shop.

When the bell rings again, she glances over the shoulder of the liquorice man and sees Jason coming in. He comes to the counter and leans against it as if the liquorice man were not there. He does not even pretend to be there for the sweets. 'Come for a walk,' he says.

'I can't,' says Nicola. 'I'm minding the shop.'

She empties the steel tray into a paper bag which she gives to the man. The bag bulges in his hands, the contents soft and dark and sweet.

Nicola's grandmother knew all about liquorice. She kept liquorice root in a wooden box in her bedroom and made liquorice tea and pennyroyal tea for the girls who went upstairs to see her. Nicola remembers wandering into her grandparents' bedroom when one of these girls was visiting. The girl was sitting on the end of the bed, on the handmade bedspread, waiting while Nicola's grandmother brewed the tea. Her grandmother put the liquorice root back in the box and, seeing Nicola as she closed the lid, said, 'This is not for you.' She steered Nicola out of the bedroom, shutting the door behind her.

A girl in Nicola's year at school was pregnant at fourteen. At the time, Nicola had never even had a boyfriend, and instead followed her teen magazines' instructions for divining the name of her future husband, combing her hair in front of a candlelit mirror so that she would see his face over her shoulder; eating salt at bedtime so that she would dream of him bringing her water. These things never worked.

'Come on,' says Jason. 'Shut the shop early.' He looks at the liquorice man, who ought to be leaving now but who is still there. Nicola, looking at Jason, would very much like to lock the door and let Jason take her to the fields, the same field in which she was lying with him on that one occasion when she was late home from school. While her granddad was waiting in the shop, doing his puzzles and expecting a break, Nicola was underneath Jason in the last remaining bit of countryside at the edge of the estate, a burst of green between this spreading estate and the next, flat on her back with her buttons undone and Jason's head blocking her view of the vast blue sky.

'My granddad might need me,' she says, although she hears the floorboards creak overhead as her granddad goes from the bathroom into his bedroom.

'He won't,' says Jason.

Nicola is waiting for the liquorice man to go. He is near the door now but still lingering, and in the end Nicola says it anyway, very quietly to Jason: 'I think I'm pregnant.'

Jason seems not to have heard. He is looking at the two

pence sweets in the tray on the counter. He chooses one and eats it standing there, and then he goes, saying that he has things to do. He leaves the wrapper and a two pence piece behind.

Her granddad will have closed his bedroom curtains. He will have taken off his shoes, and his trousers will be folded on a chair. He will be sleeping heavily in his underwear with Nicola's grandmother's handmade quilt pulled up to his chest. He won't wake up until suppertime.

Soon, Nicola will lock the empty shop and go upstairs. She will go into her granddad's room and check that he is sleeping soundly before looking through her grandmother's things, perhaps trying on the slender fifties dress, leaving the zip undone. She will run her hands over the cool glass ball. She will look inside the wooden box containing the liquorice root and the pennyroyal.

In the warm, sugary air, Nicola feels nauseous. She wonders whether she really did say it. Maybe she thought about saying it but nothing came out. Maybe she said it too quietly for Jason to hear.

The jar of liquorice is still out on the counter. She takes a piece for herself and puts it in her mouth. She is not really allowed to do that, to help herself. But she does. She must be careful not to take too much. She will take some to bed with her. She is not allowed to do that either. It stains her tongue and her saliva. When she wakes in the morning, she will first put her hands on her queasy stomach and then she will lift her head and look at her bedding, looking for dark stains.

Late

A S THE DOOR slams shut, she wonders if she has her keys. Putting her hand in her pocket, wrapping her fingers around them, she thinks of the cold key her mother used to cure hiccups. She recalls the chill of it on her skin, going down her spine, stopping her breath.

Her head is aching but not as much as it might be and she wonders if she is still drunk. She is late. She needs to be at a meeting which has already started. Her alarm clock didn't wake her. She hasn't showered or had her breakfast. She hasn't even brushed her teeth and is wearing yesterday's clothes.

She hesitates on the doorstep, squinting in the sunshine like some subterranean creature suddenly finding itself in daylight, missing her bedroom, the darkness under the duvet. She takes the few steps to her car, the key in her hand. She can feel her organs shuddering, riddled with toxins. She knows that her breath must reek of alcohol. Unlocking the car, she gets into the driver's seat and puts her face in her hands, her fingertips touching her eyelids, her breath warming her palms.

After a minute, she puts the key in the ignition and turns it but the engine only wheezes. She tries again but it will not start, and she tries again and again and again but still it will not start and once more she puts her head in her hands.

She gets out of the car, glancing up at the bedroom window, at the closed curtains. She goes to the bonnet and opens it up, looking hopelessly at the engine.

When she hears her neighbour's front door opening, she turns around. He is in his dressing gown, fetching his milk from the doorstep. He calls out to her, 'All right, Janie, love?' She opens her mouth – she might say something, tell him what has happened, ask for his help, but her tongue feels like a pound of raw liver in her mouth, and already he is shutting the door again, not waiting for an answer, no longer looking her way.

As she closes the bonnet, she notices the dirt and oil on her hands and a stain on her blouse. She is right outside her house – she could go inside and wash her hands and change her clothes but she doesn't. She locks her car and walks towards the bus stop. She is so late.

The bus, when it comes, is packed. She puts her fare in the driver's tray and he prints out her ticket and drives off before she has found a vacant seat. A large man squeezes up to make space for her, if not enough. He smiles at her as she sits down and she hopes he will not try to start a conversation.

Every time the bus turns a corner, their bodies touch, bumping against one another while she looks straight ahead. People are talking and the noise of it makes her head throb. There is a hand on her arm and someone says, 'Are you all right, dear?' but she does not look to see who has spoken and after a moment the hand is withdrawn.

She feels wretched. She drank a vast amount, working her way, with Eric, through the little recipe book which came with his fiftieth-birthday cocktail shaker. She can't begin to think how many units the two of them must have put away before she went into the bedroom and lay down without undressing. She has no idea what time that was but she knows Eric didn't come with her.

The man beside her says, 'Excuse me,' and she thinks he is going to engage her in some way, but he wants to get past her, to get off the bus. She stands and lets him out and then, worried that she might be sick, goes down to the front of the bus herself, deciding to walk the last stop, hoping that fresh air and exercise will help.

She is halfway between bus stops when she remembers her presentation. It is in her briefcase, which is still on the kitchen table where she left it the evening before. She needs it, but does not turn back.

In the foyer of the building in which she works, someone she knows holds the lift open but she takes the stairs, climbing steadily up to the fourth floor. The oily black marks have spread from her hands to her coat. She wonders whether she has touched her face and whether that is streaked too. But she does not stop at the toilets to wash her hands and check her face in the mirror and smooth her sleep-crumpled clothes. She does not stop to talk to anyone.

Going straight to the meeting room, she takes a deep breath and opens the door. There are a dozen people in there, sitting around a table, turning to look as she comes in. The door closes behind her. In the small and overheated room, she is hit by the stink of the lilies in the vase in the middle of the table, brown pollen dropping from their stamens and falling between the sections of the table onto the cream carpet. The warm stench makes her feel ill. Turning around, she hurries back out into the corridor.

She runs to the toilets and into an empty cubicle where she retches into the bowl. She stays there for a while, shaking, with her knees on cold linoleum, her hands clinging to cold porcelain.

When she comes out, the girl who takes minutes is standing there saying, 'Are you all right?' Nodding, walking past the girl, past the mirrors and the sinks, she goes out into the corridor again.

She does not go back to the meeting room but upstairs to the staff room. She rinses her mouth out in the sink and then lies down on the sofa and closes her eyes.

She hears the door opening, and someone saying, 'I think you've got the right idea, Janie.' It is a man's voice but she can't place it. She does not open her eyes. She hears him going to the little kitchen area, filling the kettle and switching it on, getting a mug from the cupboard, a teaspoon from the drawer, tapping the teaspoon against the work surface. She feels him looking at her and then he says, 'I might join you.' She doesn't respond. He says, 'Everyone's tired these days. Everyone's tired all the time. It's our environment, Janie – computers, strip lights, mobile phones. I'm tired all day but I can't sleep at night. It's light pollution and aeroplanes and all that. Can I make you a cup of tea, Janie?' After a minute, she hears him leave.

She wants to sleep but it's too bright and the fridge is noisy and the sofa is uncomfortable. She can't stop thinking about the darkened bedroom she just left.

She can still smell vomit.

There are footsteps on the stairs. When the door opens, she recognises Teresa's voice. She is saying to someone, 'Oh God, did you see that programme last night about that creature that latches onto a fish's tongue and sucks out all the blood? The tongue shrinks to nothing and the creature grows until it fills the fish's mouth. It's really grim.'

Teresa is standing near her now, standing over her, touching her shoulder and saying, 'Janie, love, are you OK? People are talking about you.' When she opens her eyes she sees that the person Teresa has come into the room with is one of the new employees, a young man. He is eating something meaty which smells bad and she begins to feel sick again.

Teresa says, 'Are you poorly?'

The young man says, 'The menopause made my mum feel tired, a bit sick.'

Janie closes her eyes again.

'And moody,' he says. 'Crabby.'

After a while, they leave.

Alone again on the sagging sofa, listening to the hum of the fridge, she has just begun to doze when the shutting door startles her.

'Janie,' says Pete, 'is everything all right? Teresa said it was the menopause.'

She has known Pete for years. He and Eric used to work together somewhere else. When they were both made redundant at the same time, Janie recommended them for positions here. Pete was hired but Eric was not.

Eric didn't really bother after that. He neither worked nor signed on. The two of them lived on her salary, and he did nothing around the house either, although he offered her endless cups of tea as if that were enough, as if that were what she wanted from him. 'If I wanted so much tea,' she said, 'I'd buy a frigging teasmade.' He got used to sleeping late and then getting slowly and cheaply drunk in front of daytime TV. When, one evening, he suggested that her hormones might be making her irritable, she said to him, 'It's not my hormones running up the heating bill. It's not my hormones stinking of cider.' At first she told him not to drink so much, not to eat so much crap, to take some exercise. 'You've already had one heart attack,' she told him. 'Are you after another?' It is a long time now, though, since she reminded him to take care of himself.

She remembers waking in the morning, reaching for him before opening her eyes, to touch his warm body.

It is, she thinks, as if a stranger came home one day instead of her husband. He wore her husband's clothes but they did not fit him and he sat on the sofa all day long with his trousers undone, and he showed little interest in sex. Their last quickie on the sofa, fuelled by cheap red wine, is more than a month old, more like two. She has become used to going to bed alone, her sleep disturbed only by the sound of the TV still on in the living room, the sound of his stumbling around or his snoring; and going to work while he is still in bed, and in the evening coming home and finding him on the sofa in front of the TV again, asking her about her day, asking her if she wants a cup of tea, touching her gently and saying, 'Janie, love, is everything all right?'

'Hey,' says Pete, sitting down on the end of the sofa, lifting up her feet and laying them in his lap, 'did you see on the telly last night about that thing that lives in snappers' mouths? That's a strange one.'

The TV was on when she got in from work. She put her briefcase down on the kitchen table, noticing the cocktail shaker and all the bottles which were out on the side. She went into the living room, where Eric was waiting with sunset-coloured cocktails. She took the glass he offered her - 'An Alabama Slammer,' he said - took a sip, ate the cherry, complimented him. Sitting down, she picked up the recipe book and leafed through it. When she finished her Alabama Slammer, she went to the kitchen and made them each a Cosmopolitan. When they'd drunk these, Eric manufactured a strong Daiquiri. She made a Gin Fizz and he made a Kamikaze. She made a Malibu Woo Woo and he made a Mojito, and at some point, perhaps after the Piña Colada, she started hurting him. Every time she opened her mouth, something horrible came out. When she went to bed, she left him in the living room surrounded by the debris of their cocktail evening.

'Janie,' says Pete, 'I think you should go home.'

She nods.

'Shall I make you a cup of tea?' he asks, already on his way to the kitchen. Emptying the still-warm kettle into two mugs, he says, 'Is Eric home? Why don't you call him, ask him to come.and get you.' He puts the tea down on the coffee table and says, 'I'll call him for you.' He speed-dials her home phone number on his mobile and passes it to her.

She listens to it ringing and then hears Eric's voice saying, 'We can't come to the phone right now.' Still she listens, and only when the recorded message ends and the answerphone beeps does she shake her head at Pete.

'We'll have our tea,' says Pete, 'and then I'm putting you in a taxi.'

She leaves her tea to go cold and refuses a taxi, but she does let Pete walk her to the bus stop. He waits with her until the bus comes and watches her get on, waving her off as if she were a brave little evacuee travelling alone for the first time in her life.

When the bus has gone three stops and is in the city centre, when she is still two miles from home, she gets off. She walks to a café she knows, somewhere she has been before with Eric.

She takes a bottle of water from the fridge, pays for it and chooses a seat by the window, looking out. It is quiet. She does not talk to anyone. There are newspapers on the tables but she does not read them. When the café begins to close, she leaves her untouched bottle of water and wanders slowly home.

Closing the front door behind her and hanging up her coat, she goes to the foot of the stairs. She does not turn to look through the living room doorway at the dirty glasses on the coffee table, at the empty sofa and the television's black screen. She climbs the stairs and enters the bedroom.

It is dark, just as it was when she left it, the curtains closed. She can still see everything though. She gets into bed. When she is ready, she reaches out. She touches Eric, his bare skin, his body, which was already cold when she woke that morning.

She closes her eyes.

No one disturbs her attempt to sleep. No one comes in asking if she wants a cup of tea. No one touches her gently and says, 'Janie, love, is everything all right?'

The Pre-War House

'The past beats inside me like a second heart.'

JOHN BANVILLE, *The Sea*

IN THE FRONT garden, in the narrow beds, the flowers which emerged in what felt like the first days of spring lie buried beneath the late snow, their opening buds like small mouths gaping in shock, their stems broken.

Inside, the rooms are full of cardboard boxes, into which the contents of the house have been packed. I open cupboards and wardrobes and drawers which I have already checked and know are empty, peering into and under the dark-wood furniture and the bare-mattressed beds, looking for the smallest thing which may have been left behind.

I remember the sounds of this house in which I grew up – the creaking of the doors and the floorboards and the stairs, the groaning of the pipes, the wheezing and sighing of the springs in the sofa cushions – the sounds of an old house aching. But mostly I remember the silence, the stillness.

Lifting the remaining pictures down from the walls, I am struck by the brightness of the squares of wallpaper behind them, the sharpness of the pattern, like pictures of the wallpaper as it used to be, framed by the wallpaper as it is now, which has faded over the years.

When the house is all packed up and everything is clean, I

will sit at the kitchen table and eat the supper I brought from home, and mark a pile of essays on the Treaty of Versailles and the Weimar Republic and the ways in which the seeds of World War Two were sown in World War One. I have bedding to put on my old single bed in my old room, in which I will sleep tonight. My car is parked in the road, in front of the garden wall, by the icy kerb, to leave the driveway free for the van which will be here tomorrow.

In the morning, the men will come, and I will let them in. They will walk through this quiet house in their heavy boots, and they will take away all the boxes and the furniture, the contents of this old house, load it all up and take it away.

'This house was brand new,' said my grandmother, 'when I was a child, in the 1930s, before the war. The garden was nothing but mud from one end to the other. My father laid the brick path down to the end wall, marked out the vegetable patch, and grassed the rest of it over.'

Little about the house had been changed since then. We were sitting on the same pre-war three-piece suite, with pre-war family photographs arranged on the pre-war furniture and pre-war pictures hanging on the high walls. Pre-war curtains kept the sunlight off the pre-war wallpaper and the pre-war carpets, and a pre-war clock ticked in the hallway.

'Over the road,' she said, 'it was all fields. They've spoilt it now, building those houses there.' She gazed out of the window at the ruined landscape. 'We knew the war was coming, and sure enough it came. I was just a girl, a little younger than you are now. One night, a bomb fell in the field opposite.' She nodded towards the new houses. 'It made a big hole in the ground, but it didn't go off. I saw it, the unex-ploded enemy bomb lying at the bottom, smooth and round like an egg in a nest.'

I thought about the quiet tree roots and the blind earth-worms, startled in the ground or torn in two, their raw ends squirming, and my grandmother looked up at the empty sky, as if she was worried that the bombs had not yet all fallen.

I imagined it still lying there, this unhatched egg buried in a hole in the ground, under the grass with the roots and the worms, under the houses, the new estate.

My father was born in the 1950s, long after the end of the war but not before the end of rationing; even in peacetime the meanness of the war lingered. He was raised by my grand-mother in this pre-war house, and it was he, in my childhood, who re-glued the wallpaper when it peeled, who mended the clock when it failed.

The front of our house, like all the other houses in the street, was painted white. Every few years, my father put on his protective overalls and spent a week up a ladder, cleaning the brickwork and the window frames, bleaching mould and treating rot and filling cracks and sanding and sealing flaking and crumbling patches. And then he painted, from left to right, from top to bottom, from corner to corner, working the new paint across each brick and between the bricks and into the corners. Our house shone in the sunshine, like the twinkling tooth in a toothpaste advert.

He liked to clean. He started in his mother's attic bedroom and cleaned all the way down to the kitchen, cleaning the windows with vinegar and newspaper, the dark wood with lemon oil, the oven with baking soda. He was like a flood washing through the house, down the stairs and out through the back door, all the dirt pouring down the drain. When he had finished, our pre-war house looked brand new.

His garden was immaculate. His lawn was like a bowling green; it looked like he trimmed it with nail scissors. Nothing wild grew there. He dealt with the seeds shat down by birds in flight, like bombs dropped by enemy planes, and the Spanish bluebells whose bulbs lay deep in the earth beneath his pristine lawn, whose shoots wormed their way towards the surface in the spring. He protected his vegetables from the cabbage maggots which wanted to burrow into the soft roots and spoil them, and from the moth larvae which wanted to lay their eggs between the young leaves of his lettuces.

Spring was a minefield; he preferred the winter, the frost, the freeze, the ice – the clean, white world.

He was not a handsome man, but he was always clean – 'spick and span,' said my grandmother – and he had strong bones, good bone structure. 'I have good bones,' he said, 'and good teeth. I have good genes.'

Like my father, I love the winter, the whitewash of snow, the freezing of everything. In deep snow, there is no garden, now gone to seed; there is no grass, grown long and uneven and littered with autumn's leaves; there are no beds, no border plants strangled by weeds; there is no driveway, no pavement, no road; there is just snow, in which the only footprints are my own.

The outside world seems remote, like a landscape photograph of the bare branches of cold trees against a blank, white sky, viewed through glass which I clean the way he did, with vinegar and newspaper.

I glue the pre-war paper where it is peeling from the walls, but I don't know how to fix the hallway clock which is running slow. I lift it down from the wall, and it keeps on ticking, pulsing in my hands.

On the whole, the only new things which came into the house came with my mother when she married my father in 1977 and in her early twenties that wasn't very much. She brought some mugs with jokes on, which were put to the back of the crockery cupboard, behind the family china, and nonetheless got broken over the years. She brought some family photographs, and displayed them on the sideboard alongside her in-laws, and my grandmother moved them to the back, these interlopers, who peeked cheerfully, colourfully, through the gaps. She brought her books, and put them in the bookcase in the living room, and my grandmother winced to see the random and vulgar paperbacks which had appeared on her shelves, which she found nestling between her hardback classics.

Before my mother married my father, she was a hostess on long-distance coaches. It wasn't well paid or glamorous – she didn't like the old-fashioned uniform or serving tea on bumpy, bendy roads – and she had never been abroad, but she got to travel up and down the country, going to cities and tourist attractions and the seaside.

My father, a passenger on a weekday coach to Bournemouth, on his way to a conference, had watched her walking up and down the aisle, with her slim figure buttoned smartly into her modest uniform, her good legs in polished heels, her long, fair hair neat, pinned up on top of her head. She had served him little disposable cups of warm tea, wobbling a little when the coach went round a roundabout, holding on, and the sunshine through the window had fallen on her face, lighting her clear skin and her blue eyes, and he had smiled, showing his good teeth.

My mother's skin was as smooth and pale as the bluebell bulbs beneath my father's lawn, as smooth and pale as the larvae in his vegetable patch.

She shaved her legs in the bath, removing the light brown stubble which sprouted from her follicles. She peered into the bathroom mirror, worrying over her complexion, looking for clogged pores and spots gathering beneath the surface, looking for the bad skin which had plagued her as a girl, looking for wrinkles and crow's feet, applying concealer and foundation and powder. She had her hair cut short now; she had it done every week, and came home from the hair salon smelling like she had been laundered.

Outside, it was nearly the twenty-first century, but when she stepped through her front door, she said, she could have been my great-grandmother stepping into her hallway sixty years earlier. She closed the door and found herself standing in a pre-war house which was deathly quiet apart from the ticking of that interminable clock. She disliked that house, with its wallpaper which was older than she was, older than my grandmother. She disliked the ancient kitchen with its pre-war china, whose gilt rims were faded from having been sucked at by generations of mouths. She wanted new cupboards and a freezer and a microwave and a mixer tap. She disliked the stillness of the house, and the smell, the smell of vinegar and mothballs – like pickled onions, she said, and death.

She once brought a new vase into the house, something

modern she liked. She put it on the mantelpiece in the living room, and my grandmother looked at it and said it didn't go. It stayed there for a while though, even after my mother found it broken on the hearth and had to glue it.

Early in their marriage, before I was born, my mother took for herself a small patch of the garden, near the end wall, where she planted a barberry bush. She sat out there from time to time, in her little bit of my father's garden, just looking at the flowers on the barberry bush, or closing her eyes in the sunshine, and my father hovered at a distance, agitated, taking it out on the weeds.

I have brought tea bags and milk and sugar, but not a mug. I unpack one of the newspaper-wrapped china cups from a cardboard box marked 'kitchen'.

There was mould growing, spores breeding on the over-ripe fruit in the fridge and in the fruit bowl, clinging to the softening skins; breeding in the bread bin and in the dregs of tea at the bottom of an unwashed cup.

The fridge is empty now, apart from my carton of milk. The bread bin and the fruit bowl and the cups are packed away, apart from the one I am using. The kettle is still out on the worktop.

There is an old bar of tar soap by the sink. Its heavy smell is unpleasant, sickening.

I turn on the tap, and the house trembles.

My sister, said my grandmother, was our mother's daughter. I had seen photographs of my mother at Susan's age, and if it hadn't been for the look of a 1960s photograph and the 1960s fashions I might not have been able to tell them apart. They had the same slight frame, the same small features, the same colouring, the same skin. They had the same tilt of the head and the same way of looking at you out of the same pair of pale blue eyes.

There was not so much of our mother in me. I was younger than my sister but bigger, and darker.

Susan had always been our father's favourite. His eyes followed her around rooms. He liked to make her laugh, to hear the laugh which was just like our mother's. And he liked to watch the night sky with her – on clear nights they went up to the attic room, sat in the dark on a bench at the window, and watched the skies through an old telescope. They sat side by side, my sister, looking at the moon and its craters, looking at the planets and the stars, looking for comets and meteors, and my father, scanning the vast, black night.

She was clever, and she knew what she wanted to do when she grew up: she wanted to study tropical diseases, parasites. She told me about worms which burrow through your eyeballs, or into your skin and lay their eggs in you, or which lay their eggs in your wounds and when the larvae hatch they tunnel into your skin to feed, and if they are disturbed they screw themselves in deeper. She told me about parasites which live in your stomach, and tiny, translucent fish in the Amazon which swim up inside you when you wee in the water, which slither up and put out their spines to anchor themselves, and start nibbling. I felt them crawling under my skin and in my stomach, felt them wriggling and chewing inside me, making me squirm.

Sometimes I went up to the attic room to look through

the telescope. I went on my own, without asking, and sat on the bench at the open window, squeezing one eye shut and looking through the eyepiece with the other. The images were blurred, distorted by thermals, seen through a heat haze. I wasn't even sure what I was looking at, these distant objects brought astonishingly close to my wide-open eye. I tried not to move or change anything, to stay still, just looking through the eyepiece; I tried to be careful.

But one time, perhaps a leg on the tripod was not fully out, or perhaps my foot moved, but as I sat there in the dark, with my eye pressed to the lens, trying to see the far-away craters of the moon, the telescope toppled, falling away from me, and when it hit the wooden floor there was a sound like something breaking inside. I sat in the dark with screwworms in my heart and flies hatching in my stomach.

I put the telescope up on its feet again and crept away, leaving the telescope broken in the darkness. I didn't tell anyone what had happened; I never told anyone it was me. When the telescope was found to be damaged, my father didn't get it mended – or perhaps he tried and found it couldn't be fixed.

In the attic, in my grandmother's old room, the windows are closed. I can't hear the outside world; I can't hear the traffic or the people going by or the neighbours' children playing in the snow.

There is a pillow on my grandmother's stripped-bare bed, and some half-finished knitting on her night-stand, something blue. I can smell her, on the pillow, in the air, in the dust.

The telescope is gone, but the bench is still there at the

window. I sit down and look out at the bright day, at the distant sky, and the tree-tops agitated by the soundless wind. I can't see the moon but it is there, lurking quietly in the daylight.

In the silence, I feel the squirming and fidgeting under my skin, in my belly.

My father worked in an office, inputting medical data and producing charts tracing the spread and control of disease. He liked the precision of statistics, the clean lines of his graphs, the capturing of epidemics and pandemics in two-tone bar charts. He worked beneath shelves full of files, shelves bowed beneath the weight of his archived records.

At home, too, he monitored activity, keeping all kinds of diaries, notebooks in which he wrote regularly. He liked to sit in the quiet corners of that quiet house, bent over his work, filling his notebooks with his small, tight writing.

He had one for the garden, in which he made notes about the various weeds and pests he endeavoured to control, about the Spanish bluebell which ruined his lawn ('naturally more invasive,' he noted, 'than the English bluebell; when cross-pollination takes place, the resulting seed is genetically corrupt'), the blackspot which attacked his roses ('fungal in-festation of the leaves, spreading to the stems and buds; no cure for the infected parts – remove and destroy'), the vine weevil which spoiled the leaves on his strawberries ('adult vine weevils are female and lay hundreds of eggs in the summer; eggs are brown and diameter is less than 1mm – very difficult to find in the soil'), and the sap-sucking aphid ('overwintering eggs are laid in crevices, and hatch in the spring').

He had one in which he documented the things he had seen through his father's telescope, looking through the attic window with my sister. While Susan was looking at the moon and the stars, looking for comets and meteors, my father was looking for UFOs, looking for flying saucers and aliens, recording anomalies in his notebook, his diary of evidence.

He had a notebook in which he monitored the activities of neighbours who encroached on his territory, whose ivy grew up the walls of his house, clamping sticky feet to his fresh paintwork and climbing up to and under his eaves; whose trees bent over the fence and dropped windfall apples on his path; whose hedges grew too high and blocked the light; whose cats crept into his vegetable patch and left their mess behind, and dug at the soil around his border plants and around the barberry bush; whose children kicked their balls onto his lawn and then came over the fence and through the hedge to fetch them back, and who put eggs through his letterbox so that they broke on his doormat, the viscous innards seeping between the fibres.

And he had one, said my mother, in which he wrote stories. He had never told her this – he kept his jottings to himself – but she had looked, and there, in one of my father's notebooks, she found stories, and in all of my father's stories, she found herself – a character who looked just the way she did, dressed the way she did, spoke the way she did; a character whose blonde hair had darkened, whose grey was coming through; a character who was wearing my mother's blue jumper and the skirt with a tear which she never got round to mending; a character who was saying something my mother had said over breakfast, something banal about the eggs. My mother was

173

furious to find herself there, to find this woman wearing her clothes and copying the things she said and her mannerisms. And in some of the stories, this woman had a daughter who was small and fair and clever, and who adored her father.

I have never kept a diary. I remember what has happened and who did what.

There are too many quiet corners in this quiet house for me. I work with the radio on, switching between stations and turning up the volume, opening windows and chasing the silence out of the emptying rooms.

In the bathroom, there is mildew in the grout between the shower tiles, and there are spiders making webs behind the toilet. I put vinegar on the mildew, but leave the spiders alone.

In some ways, I am my father's daughter, and in some ways I am not.

My mother had a friend who had a motorbike. He came by in the middle of the day, when my father was at work. You could hear the bike coming down the road, slowing outside our house, and turning in. It was noisy and smelly and the oil tank leaked.

He parked his bike in our driveway, where our father's car belonged. He took off his helmet and ran his black-leather-gloved hand through his oil-black hair. He walked, with his long-legged stride and his heavy-booted step, up to our house, to our back door, and my mother let him in.

We took our shoes off in the house, but my mother's friend didn't; he walked his dirty boots across my father's scrubbed-clean floor, and sat down at the table. My sister and I, drawn to the kitchen by the sound of the motorbike, hung around, watching him. My mother made coffee, and Susan and I were allowed to stay and have some. When my sister spooned sugar into her cup, our mother's friend said, 'You don't need sugar, you're sweet enough already,' and my sister giggled. She thought he was good-looking, although, she said, his eyes were weird, and his eyebrows met in the middle. And then he said the same thing to my mother – 'You don't need sugar,' he said, 'you're sweet enough already' – and she laughed too. I didn't like the taste of coffee, I just pretended to drink it so that I could stay, and I didn't take any sugar, and he didn't say it to me.

After a while, when my sister had finished her coffee and I had barely touched mine – just putting my lips to the rim of the cup, taking just enough to put a nasty taste in my mouth – our mother sent us outside to play. I followed Susan to the driveway, where she sat on the motorbike, first on her own and pretending to ride it, pretending to be him, and then behind me, with her arms around me, pretending to be his pillion passenger, pretending to be his girlfriend.

I liked riding the bike with my sister, but I didn't like him. I didn't like him coming to our house when my father was out. I didn't like his filthy bike standing in our driveway. I didn't like him sitting in our kitchen, making our mother laugh.

We watched them through the vinegar-clean kitchen window. We saw his hand, olive-skinned and oil-stained, touching our mother's leg underneath the table, and stroking her cheek as he stood to go.

He left dark stains on the driveway, and on our mother's pink face, and on her white jeans. She stood at the kitchen sink, scrubbing washing-up liquid into the dirty mark on her thigh.

We didn't know his name, or what he was to our mother, but we knew she'd met him a long time ago, before we were born, before she met our father. And we knew not to tell our father that he visited.

Our mother washed her face and her trousers, and our father tried to clean up the puddle of oil he found on the driveway, but it wouldn't quite go. He stood over it, troubled by the residue, the remaining stain.

I hear a motorbike. It's a sound which even now makes me go to the window. I half expect my sister to come running, to see the bike parked in the driveway, to sit on its still-warm seat. I feel her arms around me, holding on.

These motorbikes race by. When I look, it has already gone.

I sit at the kitchen table, sucking at the faded gilt rim of the china cup, drinking sugary tea – I am not yet sweet enough.

We ate in the kitchen, all together at a little Formica-topped table. I sat between my mother, with her perfect complexion and her clean, white jeans and her laundry smell, and my father, who ate slowly and carefully, leaving the skins of anything which had grown in the ground, next to the dirt and the worms. My sister sat next to our grandmother, whose jaw clicked when she ate. It was cramped around that small table, and all our elbows knocked together if we stuck them out too far.

When nobody said anything, we could just hear ourselves

eating, our cutlery against our plates, and my grandmother's jaw clicking. Sometimes my mother looked like she was going to speak, but then just raised her eyebrows instead. Sometimes my father said something like, 'A very nice piece of meat, Barbara.' And sometimes my grandmother said something like, 'Barbara's friend was here again today.'

My mother's knife squealed against her china plate.

'Barbara's friend?' said my father.

'Her friend with the motorbike,' said my grandmother.

My sister and I looked at one another, our cutlery frozen in midair, the click of our grandmother's jaw counting out the seconds like a metronome.

My father continued eating for a moment, picking away at the inside of his jacket potato, leaving its dirty skin. And then he put down his cutlery and looked at my mother, on whose clean, pink cheek I could almost see that black, oily fingerprint. He put his knife and fork together on his plate, stood up, pushed his chair under the table, and left the room.

We sat there for a while, the four of us. Only my grandmother was still eating. My mother sat opposite her, with her elbows on the table and her hands clasped together like somebody praying – *Dear God* and *In the name of Jesus Christ* – with her eyebrows raised at my grandmother, who was concentrating on her dinner, finishing off the nice piece of meat.

My mother pushed her chair back and left the kitchen. Following our father into the living room, she found him writing in one of his notebooks. Their voices carried through that quiet house, into the echoey kitchen. He said, 'I thought we agreed . . .' and, 'You did promise me, Barbara . . .' And she told him what she thought about his weird little stories, which, yes, she had read; she told him what she thought about his weird little notebook wife and his weird little notebook daughter who lived in his weird little notebook world; and my father gathered up his violated notebooks, his spoiled stories, and went upstairs.

Our mother returned to the kitchen and cleared our father's place, scraping the scraps he had left into the bin, while we ate the cold remains of our dinner.

In the kitchen, sitting alone at the table, finishing my tea, I think I hear that metronomic clicking of my grandmother's jaw, but it is just the clock ticking in a box in the hallway.

That year, my sister suddenly grew in all directions. She grew tall, taller than me and nearly as tall as our father. Breasts swelled beneath her T-shirt; blocked pores swelled beneath her skin. She was blossoming, said our mother. Our father looked at her disapprovingly, as if she were something overgrown in his carefully tended garden, a corner found going wild; as if she were something overripe in his vegetable plot, with a distasteful maturing pungency which got right up his nose.

She became mouthy and surly, arguing with him and not laughing at his jokes. She skipped meals and slammed doors, played loud music and smelt of cigarettes. She went out with boys, or brought them home. Our father would have said no, no boys, but our mother said of course there would be boys; his little girl was growing up, she said, and there would be boys.

There was no star-gazing now, through a broken telescope. My father viewed her from a distance, narrowing his eyes as if she were something unknown. He would have liked to glue her like the coming-away wallpaper, to fix her like the mind-of-its-own clock.

I don't know which was worse for him, to think that she was out there, after dark, with these boys – these boys whose bodies were pulsing with adolescent hormones, testosterone stimulating their glands, their skin erupting, their voices breaking, deepening; these boys with one-track minds and wandering hands – or to know that these boys were in his house, their enormous shoes in his hallway.

Susan and I shared a bedroom. When she had friends round, I sat in the living room with my father and my grandmother, doing homework or reading in dimming light or beneath the fringed and floral standard lamp, listening to the clicking of my grandmother's knitting needles, and, through the ceiling, the bass beat, the heartbeat thump, of Susan's music, and the deeper tones of a boy's voice. My mother did not sit with us. She moved about the house, singing to herself, or she went out. My father sat in his armchair, waiting for bedtime, trying not to think about the boys and their hormones and their wandering hands, waiting for his wife to come home.

My mother often came home smelling of smoke. It clung to her coat and her clothes; it clung to her hair and her night-air-flushed skin and her breath. It followed her in through the kitchen door and crept through the house.

I stand on the doorstep, letting in some fresh air. It is icy out. I can see my breath, like when we used to hold imaginary cigarettes between our fingers and pretend we were puffing out smoke, when we were little, when it was cold.

I don't smoke, but sometimes I like the smell of it, the smell of my sister's skin, the smell of my mother coming home.

Spring spoiled my father's garden with beautiful weeds. The Spanish bluebells erupted from the earth, worming up into the light, a bank of them invading and desecrating his flawless lawn. Even as my mother admired them, my father pulled them up, though the fecund bulbs remained, deep down in the soil.

Where the bluebells had been, there were holes and bare patches, and my father cut the grass brutally short, punishing his ravaged lawn.

In his vegetable patch, he found his neat rows of seedlings turned over and broken beneath the weight of cat shit, turds planted and raked over as if they might bloom come summer. He found cabbage maggot pupae in the soil around his leaf vegetables, and moth larvae eggs between the leaves of his good lettuces, and he crushed them between his fingers to stop them hatching.

He found oily fingerprints on the wallpaper, and tiny woodworm holes in the skirting boards, small piles of frass beneath them, and in one corner of the kitchen he found the little black droppings of a rodent. In the cupboard, there was a cereal packet with a hole in the side, cornflakes spilling out. He put these things in the bin: the insect shit and the rodent shit and the spoiled cereal packet at which sharp little teeth had gnawed, the tiny evidence of intrusion and contamination. The oily fingerprints remained, ingrained.

He set a trap, an old-fashioned mouse-trap with a sprung metal jaw. At night, I heard the little scrabbling sounds of something ferreting about in the kitchen, and silence, such tiny silences, and I stiffened, imagining the baited jaw, waiting for the snap of the trap, the damage.

In the morning, my father stood in the middle of the kitchen, beneath the strip light, holding the mouse, which he had found caught in his trap, lying bloody and broken and struggling on his kitchen floor, its smooth, pink tail writhing like a worm.

My grandmother sat at the table, eating her breakfast and eyeing the mouse. 'That won't be it,' she said. 'That won't be all. There'll be a nest somewhere.' Once again, the trap was set, the sprung metal jaw baited, tense, and once again, I held my breath.

My father took the mouse out to the dustbin, and stood there for a minute, with the chill of early spring, the chill of the outside world, on his skin and in his lungs and beneath his slippered feet, its brightness in his eyes. There was fresh oil on the driveway, new dark puddles next to the stains he had tried to scrub away.

It is February now, and there are no doubt grubs in my father's vegetable plot; the insects have no doubt been making themselves at home, the females laying their eggs in his soil, the maggots hatching and burrowing down and eating through the roots of the cabbages he planted in the autumn, the pupae overwintering underground, waiting to emerge as flies in the spring.

One weekend in the middle of the summer, the motorbike appeared in our driveway again. It was a Saturday and my father was at home. He was in the back garden, mowing stripes into the lawn. I was at the front of the house, sitting on the well-scrubbed doorstep, swatting at the flies and looking at my mother's friend sitting on his motorbike, the engine running.

The front door opened. I fell inwards a little, and my mother came out. She had to step over me, her heeled sandals and her bare legs clearing me, her hand lightly touching my head, the hem of her skirt and her perfume breezing by. She cut across the corner of the front garden, her heels sinking into the grass, making holes in the lawn, and clicking down the driveway to the motorbike. She climbed up behind her friend and was whisked away, riding pillion without a helmet, her bare knees gripping his hips, the flimsy fabric of her skirt catching the wind they made, as my father appeared at the side of the house, holding nettles in his gloved hands.

We watched them go, and even when they were long gone, it seemed as if the black fumes still hung in the air, and the sound of the engine still throbbed in our ears, and the sensation of her passing fingertips still lingered in my hair, at the roots.

My grandmother made dinner, a salad with cold cuts. We ate with the door and the windows open, until the kitchen filled with flies, and then with the door and the windows closed, despite the heat, the closeness, and the flies which were already in.

My mother came home in the small hours. The motorbike lingered in our driveway, disturbing us, polluting the clear, night air. When her friend rode away, my mother came in, through the kitchen door – I heard the squeal of her key turning in the lock, the creak of the stairs, the throb of the water pipes, the complaining of the ageing house woken in the middle of the night. I heard my father's voice, my mother's name ('Barbara,' he said, 'Barbara, Barbara . . .'). And then there was silence, and I held my breath.

My mother's friend appeared every few weeks after that, and took her away for the day and sometimes overnight, and it seems to me we spent that whole summer just waiting for his motorbike to appear, just waiting for her to leave.

In the winter, ice forms inside the pipes and sometimes they burst.

There is a programme on the radio about the history of quarantine, about ships anchored and isolated to prevent the spread of the plague – forty days and forty nights of confinement, floating, away from the world, just waiting. Or cholera, and I imagine the waiting, with a parasite deep in the intestines, with an eye on the bowels, the waiting and watching.

My father stood at the kitchen sink, frowning at the summer's flies which lay dying or dead on the windowsill, frowning at the things on the draining board which had been washed up but were not clean – one of the good teacups with the rose-pink stain of my mother's lipstick on the rim, and a dirty tumbler which he held up to the light, peering at the greasy fingerprints on the glass.

The lawn was littered with fallen leaves, our gutters clogged with decomposing debris. That year, the snow came early, and any leaves which hadn't been raked up lay beneath it, freezing.

My mother left, with her belongings, everything she wanted, in one small suitcase. She took her modern vase, and she left us; she left her barberry bush, and her footprints in the snow on the driveway, walking away. Where her footsteps stopped, there was a motorbike track, and oil in the snow.

My father cut down the barberry bush, cut it right down to the ground.

If we went out, walking briskly, he eyed the frontages of the neighbours' houses, the paintwork as dingy as decaying teeth, net curtains yellowing like jaundiced eyes, weeds flourishing in the overgrown lawns and sprouting through the cracks in the paths. He eyed the dog mess burning holes in the snow on the pavement, and the greying slush in the gutters, the street soiled beneath his feet, defaced.

When the gossiping neighbours saw us they snapped shut their mouths, cutting off the ends of their sentences, the unspoken scraps squirming on their tongues like halved earthworms in the dirt.

My father came home and shut the front door with one shoulder against it, and locked it, as if the outside world were a cupboard full of so much crap.

He ignored the phone when it rang. He stood in the hallway looking at it, and didn't pick it up. Perhaps he thought it might be my mother, asking to come home. Perhaps he was afraid that it was not.

I tried to find some trace of her, but I found none, not even a cheap romance in my grandmother's bookcase, or a mug with a joke on it at the back of the kitchen cupboard; not even the colour of her mouth on the side of an old teacup, or the smell of her in the drawers where her clothes had been or in the bathroom cabinet where she had kept her toiletries.

My grandmother made supper, and we all ate together

at the little kitchen table, while fresh snow settled, and the pre-war clock ticked in the hallway.

I step out of the back door and walk down to the end of the garden, leaving my footprints in the snow on the lawn, treading carefully on the icy path.

There is a spent firework and evidence of cats in the vegetable patch. The barberry bush has grown back; it is almost up to my shoulders. There is something here of my mother's after all, something she left behind, something she may or may not have wanted.

'Not long now,' says the next door neighbour, who has followed me down to the end of the garden on his side, and is leaning on the fence.

'No,' I say, 'not long now.' I want him to go away, but he stays where he is, looking at me.

'Sorry to hear about your father passing away.' *Passing away*, he says, the euphemism as light and clean as falling snow.

'Thank you,' I say.

'My wife and I used to call on him,' he says. 'We were sure he was in, but he never answered the door. He used to keep his curtains closed, during the day.'

The insinuation hangs between us. He stands there, with his arms dangling over the fence like the branches of his apple tree, dropping unwanted fruit into my father's garden where it rots, attracting wasps.

'He never got over it, did he?' he says. 'He was never quite right after that.'

I turn away. Beneath the barberry bush, in the lee of the

wall, the ground is bare, snowless, and stray flowers have taken root in the cold earth. They have a strong smell, these wild plants, and even when I walk away, back up to the house, the scent follows me.

When the snow melted, autumn's dead and unraked leaves were still there underneath, rotting on the lawn, and the oil stains remained on the driveway.

My father raked up the stray leaves. I watched him from the house, pulling his rake across his thawing lawn, and standing, staring at the grass beneath his feet, as if it were not just grass, as if this were not his perfect lawn, as if it were something strange. I watched him go down to his shed and return with a spade. Its clean metal caught the cold sunlight, its glint dazzling me. In the chill of that pre-spring day, he touched the sharp edge of his spade to his perfect lawn, raised his foot and stamped on the tread, driving the head into the ground. He lifted metres of turf, turned over tons of earth, digging out the bluebell bulbs one by one. It took him days. He turned the lawn into mud; it must have been almost as it was when my great-grandfather first stood there, wondering where to begin. At night, the garden was a strange barren moonscape. The discarded bulbs lay in buckets, their roots drying, their shoots wilting.

When he was done, when he was certain that every last bulb was out, that nothing remained, he levelled the earth and replaced the turf and made his lawn immaculate again. He stood back, resting his spade and his aching body, the light going, his sweat turning cold.

But he left alone that part of the garden which my mother

once took for herself; he didn't go digging there, removing the turf and turning over the earth beneath the end wall. That shady patch he just kept as neat as he could, keeping the grass clipped short and that resilient barberry bush cut down to the ground.

In the spring, cabbage maggots hatched from their over-wintering cocoons and laid eggs in my father's vegetable patch, and he pored through the soil, hunting out these nests and crushing the small, white eggs. Slug eggs laid in the autumn hatched, and he found holes in the leaves of new plants, seed-lings ruined. He buried beer traps in the ground, jars in which to drown the slugs which ate their way through his garden at night. I stood nearby, watching, and he turned to me and said, 'We used to drown kittens, the unwanted litters of cats on heat.'

Bluebells still come up, every spring. They are not yet out this year, but the bulbs are down there, deep in the earth, their green shoots aching for the daylight.

And there are eggs, buried in the soil, waiting for warmer weather, when they will hatch.

My grandmother sat in her armchair keeping her hands busy with knitting, keeping her tongue busy with boiled sweets. When she wasn't knitting, her hands trembled, and when she wasn't sucking on sweets, her tongue loosened.

She always gave up sweets for the forty days of Lent. It made her feel good, she said; it made her feel clean.

'Your father too,' she said. 'He won't have sweets now until Easter.' We were sitting in the living room and she had her knitting basket out. She was unpicking an old blue jumper for the wool. Taking her little scissors to where it had been bound off, and cutting through, she said, 'Your mother, on the other hand, she just ate whatever she liked; she never gave up anything.' She pulled at the neat rows of stitching, pulling the wool loose. 'Always did just as she pleased,' she said. 'And what your father gave up for her. When your father met your mother, he was engaged to a lovely girl.'

While she talked, I gathered up the unravelling wool, balling it, trying to keep it neat. My grandmother unpicked a white button at the neck, and I realised that this was my mother's blue jumper, losing its shape and coming apart in her hands.

'There,' she said, 'all done,' and we sat there holding my mother's jumper, which was just a ball of second-hand wool in my hands, and a loose button placed in a box in my grandmother's knitting basket, beside her sharp little scissors.

It is the first day of Lent today. I don't know what I would give up. I have never drunk much, though sometimes I still find the reek in my nostrils. I don't smoke, though as I say, sometimes I do like the smell – but I have seen the pictures of lungs coated with tar, stained black, suffocating; I have seen the yellowing skin.

I could give up the sugar I take in my tea, but I won't. I drop a sugar cube into the cup, into the hot tea, and stir it until it dissolves.

'Stop looking at me,' said Susan.

'I wasn't looking at you,' I said, 'I was looking out of the window.'

We were in our bedroom, lying on our beds. Susan's bed was right underneath the window, and mine was opposite. I had been looking out of the window, at Sunday's steady rainfall, but I had also been looking at her. Not having a picture of our mother – the few there had been having gone –I sometimes tried to catch a glimpse of her by looking at my sister.

'Stop it,' she said, wafting her hand, as if she could feel my eyes crawling over her face. She turned onto her side, away from me, and as she turned I saw a red mark, a bruise on her neck, blood vessels burst beneath her skin, a love-bite. And then, with her face to the wall, she said, 'Your eyes are weird.'

The rain hammered down outside.

She wanted her own bedroom; she said so all the time, even though there was no spare room, and even though I always left when she wanted the room to herself, and sat downstairs while her friends sat on my bed and touched and used my things. When they left, when I returned to my room, I found my bedding crumpled, and the shape of someone's bottom or evidence of feet on my pillow; I found brown curls of tobacco on the covers of my books, and the corners of pages, neat little rectangles, torn out, and the air smelt like my father's bonfires, his piles of burning leaves.

I run the vacuum cleaner into my father's bedroom, sucking dust from the spaces between the bare floorboards.

I hoover through into our old bedroom, pushing the nose of the vacuum cleaner underneath my sister's bed, and it strains into the empty corners like a bloodhound on a leash, recognising a scent which is scarcely there. Her bare mattress sags in the middle, the broken springs forming a hollow which remembers the shape of her, the weight of her.

There was blood on my pyjama bottoms, on the yellow cotton bed sheet, on the mattress underneath.

My grandmother told me not to wash my hair or have a bath for a week. I was unclean, like an Old Testament woman who was not allowed to touch food because she would contaminate it, the bread and butter and fruit she touched spoiling, the meat rotting and the wine turning to vinegar.

I was a young woman now, she said, and must be careful. She said this to my sister too, 'You have to be careful.'

I studied my face in the mirror, looking for my mother but not finding her, looking for my father, but my bones were not his. I peered, looking for eyebrows which met in the middle, looking at my weird eyes staring back.

I ate more, eating between meals, a habit of which my father disapproved; it showed a lack of discipline. He found me in the kitchen, and looked at me as if I were a pest he had found in his cupboards, getting at his food.

I clean the kitchen floor, scrubbing at the tiles which are not really dirty, scrubbing away footprints which aren't there.

I pour my bucket of water down the drain by the back door, empty the vacuum cleaner's dust bag, and take the rubbish out down the side of the house to the dustbin at the front.

I wash my hands with the foul tar soap and put the kettle on. In the bare kitchen, I sit down at the small table and eat my sandwiches, and the bread and butter and tomatoes do not spoil at my touch and the meat does not rot, and the water comes to a furious boil in the corner.

Most of the time, my father was out, at work or in the garden; or he was busy in some quiet part of the house, cleaning or writing in his notebooks; or he was sleeping.

Sometimes he slept during the day when he was supposed to be at work. And sometimes he stayed awake at night – I heard him downstairs, in the kitchen, looking for mice, or saw him standing in the garden, down by the end wall, in the moonlight.

Either way, we hardly saw him, apart from at mealtimes, when he looked at my sister and me the same way he looked at his vegetable patch in the spring, as if there might be something unpleasant in there, some unwanted interloper; the same way he looked at the skins of the vegetables on his plate, as if they were unclean.

'You,' he said, over dinner, 'do not have good bones.' It was not clear whether he meant me or Susan or both of us. We all kept eating. 'You,' he continued, pointing his knife at my sister, 'are all Barbara. You,' he said, pivoting the knife slowly like a sniper's rifle, turning the blade towards me, 'I don't know.'

I read his notebooks, and saw what he had done to my mother. He had removed the darker shades and the grey from her hair; he had grown her blond hair long again, pinning it neatly on top of her head. He had stitched up the tear in her skirt. And he had removed her child. He had made her as she used to be; he had made her young and smart and childless, and still in love with him.

He discarded things which belonged to my sister and me, as if we were no longer there. Our belongings went missing and turned up in the dustbin. We found our wardrobes empty, the hangers bare, our clothes put out on the front step for charity, waiting to be taken away. We brought these things inside again, put them back where they belonged, and if my father looked he would find them still there, returning and returning like the endlessly blooming bluebells and the endlessly breeding insects.

Sitting at the kitchen table marking essays, one-thousand-word assignments summarising the conclusion of one war and the beginnings of the next, I watch the stretched-tight skin of my distended belly pulsating, the baby moving inside me. The rhythmic kicks, or maybe hiccups, feel and look like an enormous heart beating in my stomach. Now and again, something comes to the surface, the shape of an elbow or a knee beneath my skin, pushing up inside me.

I remember the nausea, like seasickness, the barely-there watery vomit spat into the toilet bowl, my bare knees on the cold linoleum.

I have heard a heartbeat, beating fast like a bird or a mouse.

'No,' I said.

Susan stood in the bedroom doorway. There was a boy behind her, on the landing. 'Go on,' she said.

'No,' I said, 'I'm busy. And I was here first.' I was reading, something for school. I could have read downstairs, and there was nobody down there – our father was out and our grandmother was quiet, probably napping, in her attic room – but

I didn't like the boy my sister was with. I had met him in the kitchen once – he came in through the back door, bringing with him a cloying smell of weed. I didn't like his lingering, clinging look, his long fingers stroking the roll-up he was making, bits of tobacco dropping onto the kitchen floor.

'All right then,' she said, and went back out onto the landing, pulling the door to behind her. I listened for the sound of their footsteps on the stairs, my sister and this boy going down to the kitchen or the living room, but instead I heard the sound of my father's bedroom door opening, and closing.

I sat on my bed, staring at my book, reading the same page over and over again to the heartbeat thump of the headboard against the wall.

After about an hour, they came out and went downstairs. They had picked up their clothes and their cigarettes; they had made the bed. They had left the room just as it was, except perhaps for the stray brown curls on the bedding, and that pervading smell of smoke.

It is late now. I open the back door for some night air before locking up. There is a full moon, hanging heavy and milky in the dark sky. It lights the snow on the lawn and the ice on the path and the high, white walls of this pre-war house.

In the snow I see my footprints, and a bluebell, the tips of its strong, green leaves just poking through, emerging into the cold night. I imagine my father standing over his lawn, amazed to see them still coming through after all that.

I'm blooming, apparently. You're blooming, they say, as if I am a seasonal shrub.

I swear I can smell the barberry bush and the wild flowers, the weeds, all the way from the end of the garden.

From time to time, my father found my sister loitering in the town centre with her friends, with boys, during the day, during the week, when she should have been at school or coming home. What was she doing, he wanted to know, hanging about in the street like a stray cat, with all these randy toms sniffing around her. Well what was *he* doing there, she said, spying on her, bothering her, when he should have been at work. And what's more he stank, she said, he reeked.

He tried to keep her in the house in the evenings, but he couldn't make her stay; she kept slipping away.

He smelt the smoke on her breath and in our bedroom. He found dog-ends in her pockets. Well, what was he doing looking, she asked; what was he doing going through her pockets; what was he doing in her bedroom? What had *she* been doing, he replied, in *his* bedroom? She smoked in the house and in the street, and she looked, said our father, like a slut.

They sat across the kitchen table from one another, my father and my sister. Every morning over breakfast and every evening over dinner, my father sat opposite my sister and saw my mother glaring at him through my sister's cold blue eyes. He saw Barbara twenty years younger, before us, before him; he saw Barbara with her good figure and the bad skin of her adolescence; he saw Barbara in her youth, stinking of smoke and going with boys and telling him to go to hell.

He washed out her filthy mouth with tar soap, with his hand squeezing the back of her neck, holding her hard, pushing her head forward over the sink. The smell of that tar soap was like tasting it, that thick, burnt smell in my nostrils, in my throat, in my stomach. And when he let her go, or when she struggled free, there were red marks where he had held her, the imprints of his fingers on her skin.

Sometimes, when I try to picture my sister, when I try to see her face, all I can see is those cold, blue eyes. And sometimes I don't see her face at all – I see her lying on her side, turned to the wall, the blood vessels in her neck broken.

My father cleaned his car as fastidiously as he cleaned the house. His car was gunmetal grey, with immaculate bodywork which he washed every week in the driveway, chasing away the warm, dirty suds with cold, clean water, chasing them over the roof and the bonnet and down the sides of the car, down the driveway, over the pavement, into the gutter and down the drain. He cleaned the inside of the car, polishing the dashboard and the windscreen and the mirrors, and hoovering the carpeting and the upholstery, pushing the nozzle of the vacuum cleaner into the corners and crannies and sucking out the dirt, and taking out the odd empty bottle which rolled about under his seat, on the floor of his clean car, and putting it in the dustbin.

There was often a bottle or two under the sink, with the cleaning products, behind the bleach.

There were bottles in the garden shed. We were not allowed to go in my father's shed, but I did. Inside, his garden tools hung spick and span from nails on the walls; he always cleaned his tools after using them, and then hung the right tool back up on the right nail. There were magazines, in a neat pile on a high shelf. There was a bicycle, my mother's old bicycle, dirty and rusting, its tyres deflated, under an old sheet. And there were bottles, half-full or empty, up on the shelf next to the magazines.

There were bottles in his bedroom, under his bed and on his windowsill, behind the curtain. They rattled when my father moved about at night, trembling on the floorboards and against the cold window.

My father's breath over the breakfast table smelt bad, like something dead or dying. It seeped from his skin, that death or dying; it seeped from his pores and from the rims of his discoloured eyes.

I can see the garden shed from the window of my old bedroom. Even the shed is empty now, everything has been packed up or thrown away. There is ivy, though, growing through the roof, pushing its way beneath the roofing felt and between the planks, pushing through the webs the spiders have made.

I lay a clean double sheet over the mattress of my old single bed. I haven't brought a pillow so I use the one I found in my grandmother's room. Lying down, breathing in, trying to smell a laundry smell, I smell my grandmother, vinegar and dust.

There are no curtains at the window. I turn on my side and close my eyes. When I open them again, I am aching with hunger, and the moon is a huge, bright hole in the vast, black night, in the sky full of stars and comets and meteors, and the aliens my father always thought were coming.

I drifted through the long summer, through the unbroken stretch of eventless days. There was no school until September, no holiday by the sea. There was no rain for weeks on end, and the dry grass turned yellow in the parched garden. I slept badly at night; it was close.

There were men resurfacing the road in front of our house. For weeks the screaming noise of their machinery and their shouting over the noise and the thick smell of hot tarmac filled the still air. They moved slowly up the road in their heavy boots, with their heavy machines, and the road they left behind them was immaculate.

One morning, when my sister was not at home and my father was out at work, I went to his shed. I touched the tools hanging from nails on the walls, leaving prints on the cleaned and polished metal. I looked at his magazines, at the naked women with their legs wide open. I unscrewed the tops of the half-full and empty bottles and smelt the poisonous fumes which escaped from their necks. The sun beat through the little plastic window into the airless shed, and I felt grubby, my pores full of heat and filth.

I took the sheet off the bicycle and wheeled it out onto the path. It was a sad thing, a sit-up-and-beg bike with a little bell. I cleaned its dirty frame and inflated its flat tyres and oiled its rusty chain. And then I put it back in the shed, under the sheet.

Susan was often out of the house, with her friends. Mostly she came home for the dinners our grandmother made, but sometimes she stayed out all night while my father waited for her downstairs.

And sometimes, Susan stayed home all day with me. We sunbathed on the lawn like two hot cats. We lay on our backs, with the grass and the daisies pressing into our bare skin, and the hot sun pushing down on the lids of our closed eyes.

'*Nosema ocularum*,' she said. 'Lives underground, in the earth, and in hot weather it tunnels up to the surface and jumps in your ear and wriggles into your brain and eats its way out through your eyeballs.' She poked a blade of grass into my earhole and tickled the little hairs, making me shudder.

'*Wohlfahrtia magnifica*,' she said. 'Lives in your underwear drawer, in your gussets, and when you pull up your pants it crawls up your bumhole and you fart yourself to death.'

I stand up, and feel the bulging pressure in my abdomen, the weight of the nesting baby and the tensing of my body readying itself. I go to the bathroom, and then lie awake in the small hours listening to the tired pulsing of the old pipes.

I once flew over Russia, and through the window I thought I saw an endless cloudscape far below, its white streaked with grey, and then realised that it was land, the bleak sprawl of Siberia.

Sometimes, now, I have trouble sleeping.

Cerebrum vermiculus. Lives in your brain, and crawls through your eyes, and eats its way through your heart.

We were sitting on the front wall, baking in the midday sun. We had been there all morning with nothing else to do. The bricks were hot under the palms of my hands and through the seat of my shorts and against my bare heels, which I bounced against the wall, marking time. It was the longest day.

Susan lit a cigarette, and I imagined the tarry heat filling her mouth, her throat, her lungs. She had another love-bite on her neck, a bruise blooming under her skin.

I said, 'I found Mum's old bike in the shed.'

Susan said nothing, glanced down at the cigarette burning between her fingers.

'I fixed it up.'

She shrugged. She turned and looked down the road, gazing into the empty day, into the heat haze which hovered over the road, buckling the clean lines, shimmering like a desert horizon in a film just before a mirage appears. She sucked at her cigarette, her cheeks hollowing.

I hopped off the wall and went down by the side of the house into the back garden, over the bone-dry lawn and down the hot brick path to the airless shed, and fetched out my mother's old bicycle. I wheeled it up to the front of the house and stood it on its stand, the soles of my bare feet cooking on the oily driveway.

'Let's go for a ride,' I said. 'I'll pedal.'

Susan looked at the bicycle. I rang the bell and she smiled. She stubbed out her cigarette on the wall, flicked the dog-end into the flower bed behind her, and dropped her feet down onto the pavement. 'Okay,' she said.

I held the handlebars and straddled the bike, and she climbed on behind me and held on. I could feel her weight, and wobbled at first, unbalanced. We weaved out of the driveway, the handlebars scraping against the front wall. We bumped down the kerb and onto the melting road. We rode up and down, getting steadier and faster, up and down and turning at each end of the street, arcing through the shimmering horizon, like we were the mirage in the desert, Susan's summer dress catching the wind we made, baring her pale legs.

I saw our father's car turning into the street, the sun's dazzling glint on its clean bodywork. We were cycling towards the house, unsteadily but still fast enough to make wind, and he was driving towards us, into the sun, which was beating through his shiny windscreen, beating into his red-rimmed eyes, and empty bottles were clinking, rolling around, on the vacuum-cleaned floor of his car.

For a moment, there was nothing, just the slow, hot day, and the almost empty road, and the sun touching the gleaming bonnet of my father's car and bouncing off, and then there was a dreadful sound, like something snapping, and the heavy, burnt smell of tar.

Standing slowly, standing in the middle of the road, in the middle of that endless day, in the middle of that sprawling summer, I saw my sister, lying on her side on the pavement, on the slabs, the swell of blood beneath her skin, her cold, blue eyes turned to the wall.

My father, out of the car, stood back, his sweat turning cold. The stink of burnt rubber hung in the air. The dark streaks of his tyres stained the brand-new road.

I touch the scars on the insides of my arms and on my legs, where the tarmac took the skin off, where scabs formed and then peeled away, brown and brittle like dead leaves in the autumn.

At night, I still find myself frozen in that long moment, that timeless limbo. I still hear that silence, such a silence, and then the snap, the damage.

❧

I wash my face in the bathroom sink, splashing cold water against my tired skin.

Every last thing is now packed in the boxes, which are marked up and sealed and ready to go. The cupboards and wardrobes and drawers are empty. The walls are bare. The fridge is switched off, the door ajar. Nothing has been left behind under the dark-wood furniture or the bare-mattressed beds. Everything is clean.

The things I brought with me are out in my car, ready to go home.

It is early. Peter won't be up yet. He will be in our bed, and our bed will be warm, even though it is cold outside.

There is knocking at the front door, knocking and ringing and voices. From the top of the stairs I can see a figure on the doorstep, the shape fractured by the glass, a head pressing close, hands cupped around the eyes, trying to see through into the naked hallway. The men are here.

While they empty the house, I take one last walk through the garden, down to the end wall, to the barberry bush.

I have put in my bag the half-finished knitting I found on my grandmother's night-stand, the beginnings of a very small jumper made out of the blue wool she unravelled that day in Lent, which I wound into a small, tight ball while she talked.

'When your father met your mother,' she said, 'he was engaged to a lovely girl.'

My mother, at that time, was also spoken for; she had a boy-friend, a good-looking young man with olive skin and oil-black hair and eyebrows which met in the middle. She was eight weeks pregnant, but not yet showing, and she had not yet told anyone, not even her boyfriend, the father.

That summer, after the trip my father made to Bournemouth for a conference, he took the same coach to the coast and back every few weeks, on his own, just to see my mother, to be handed those warm cups of tea. And half the time the hostess he found on that seaside-bound coach was not my mother, who was on another coach going somewhere else, or she was with her good-looking boyfriend, or not, because he left her when she started to show.

On the last coach trip he made, my father took his tea from my mother and smiled, and asked her, if she was free, if she would like to, if she had time to look around Bournemouth.

He left his fiancée and married my mother, who wore white over her bump, and he brought her home, to his mother's house.

When the baby was stillborn, my mother dug a small grave at the end of the garden, by the wall, and laid her baby in it, in a shroud at the bottom of that hole, like an egg in a nest. She filled in the hole and planted a barberry bush, and my father clipped and weeded the grassed-over grave and made it neat.

Now, in the long grass, wild flowers flourish, their roots reaching for those tiny bones. Fly larvae have been nibbling at my father's vegetables, and beetle larvae have been nibbling at the woodwork, and moth larvae have been nibbling at my grandmother's clothes, which are inside the boxes being carried through the front door by the men, and I hear the slow ticking, the metronomic clicking, of the hallway clock going by.

The empty house has a hollow echo. It must be almost as it was when my great-grandmother first walked through the front door, stepping into the hallway of her brand-new pre-war house.

When the van has left, I lock the front door behind me and walk down the driveway to my car, and the footprints I make are lost amongst all the other footprints, the men's big bootprints, coming and going in the snow.

This book has been typeset by
SALT PUBLISHING LIMITED
using Neacademia, a font designed by Sergei Egorov
for the Rosetta Type Foundry in the Czech Republic.
It is manufactured using Creamy 70gsm, a Forest
Stewardship Council™ certified paper from Stora Enso's
Anjala Mill in Finland. It was printed and bound by
Clays Limited in Bungay, Suffolk, Great Britain.

CROMER, NORFOLK
GREAT BRITAIN
MMXVI